THE RAT WAR

THE RAT WAR

Elsie McCutcheon

Farrar Straus Giroux
New York

Contents

For Jim and my mother, with thanks

1

York to Saxford

"The War Is Not Over!" the poster on the door of the station waiting room blared in letters the colour of blood.

Nicholas felt ice-needles prick the back of his neck. There was a sudden hot drumming in his ears. The war was not over! Was it true? It must be if that poster had been fixed up there. How terrible! All those celebrations last year—the bonfires, the street parties, the fireworks—they had all been a mistake then.

He could not see the name of the station anywhere so he had only a rough idea of where they were—somewhere between London and Suffolk. He did know, though, that by now they must be far away from York, so probably Bridget and Gramarye had not heard about the war not being finished after all. Bridget wasn't very good about news at the best of times, and poor Gramarye, lying in bed like a log, had to depend on her now that he and Morna had left. How could they tell them? Should they jump off the train and start making their way back to York?

He leaned over to grab the hem of Morna's coat and shook it agitatedly.

"What is it now?" she asked crossly. She had not yet recovered from her humiliation at Liverpool Street Station when Bridget had asked the woman in the opposite corner of the compartment to keep an eye on them.

"Look!" he commanded, pointing tragically towards the notice. "It says the war's not over after all, Morna. Whatever are we going to do? We must let Gramarye know."

The guard blew his whistle as Morna, startled, pressed her face against the window to look in the direction of Nicholas's pointing finger. Then her high, mocking laugh rang out above the energetic panting of the slowly moving train.

"Oh, Nick!" she exclaimed. "You are a ninny! Can't you see what it says beneath the large letters?" Then knowing that he could not because he was not wearing his spectacles, she read aloud, "Your New Enemy Is The Rat! Help Destroy It!"

"Oh, gosh! Thank goodness!" Nicholas fell back into his seat. The feeling of relief was so warm and cushiony, he did not care that he had made a fool of himself.

The woman who had been asked to keep an eye on them looked up from her knitting. "Bless his heart!" she said.

There were only the three of them in the compartment, and now that the silence had been broken she seemed determined to find out all about them. She began with a thoughtful, "So you're going to your aunt's, are you?" (for Bridget had told her that), then added a casual, "Now why would that be?"

Morna, never reluctant to tell their story, tossed her beribboned plaits back and sat up importantly. "Well, we were sent home from India in 1939 to live with our grandmother in York," she began. "Our father's a major in the army out there, you see."

"From India!" the woman exclaimed.

"We were the youngest passengers on the ship," Morna continued. "I was four and Nick was only two. Of course there were nurses and people to look after us . . ."

"Still! From India!" the woman repeated admiringly.

"We've been with Gramarye from then until today—Nick called her Gramarye when he was two. He was trying to say 'Grandma Mary' and our grandmother said she rather liked it because it meant 'enchantment'—Bridget, the old lady you saw at the station, is Gramarye's companion. She came on the train with us this morning as far as London. Mrs Rawlinson-Fox, Gramarye's neighbour, said she would sit with Gramarye until Bridget got back. Gramarye had a stroke, you see, two weeks ago."

"Oh, dear, I am sorry," said the woman. "How terrible!"

"Yes," said Morna. "It was especially terrible for Nick. He was the one who found Gramarye lying unconscious at the foot of the stairs. So now we have to go and live with our Aunt Dorothy in Suffolk until our parents come home in September."

2

"Gramarye is getting better, though," Nicholas put in quickly, uneasy at the dark turn the conversation had taken.

"Oh yes," agreed Morna. "We might have stayed. But Bridget wanted to be rid of us. She's old and rather peculiar," she added.

"She would have kept me," Nicholas pointed out. "She said so."

"Yes," said Morna with a bitter little twist of the lips. "She likes people who don't have minds of their own."

"You're only saying that because of your liberty-bodice!" Nicholas retorted, stung.

He looked at the knitting-lady. "Morna was fearfully rude to Bridget this morning," he explained, "because Bridget said she must wear her grey woollen stockings and her liberty-bodice for such a long journey."

"In June, on a sunny day like this!" exclaimed the woman.

"Exactly!" said Morna. "Wasn't it ridiculous? I wouldn't, though."

"Quite right, too," said the woman. "Good for you!"

Morna sat back, clear-browed, smiling out of the window, and Nicholas looked at her admiringly. He would never have dared criticize one grown-up to another. But if Morna was sure she was in the right, she never held back, no matter to whom she was talking. Gramarye said she was a true Newton —a natural leader like their father, Major Newton, and their grandfather, Colonel Newton, who had been Gramarye's husband.

Nicholas was not a true Newton, although he tried hard to behave as though he were. It was only with Morna's help that he was able to keep up the pretence.

He still remembered how terrified he had been of Gramarye's two table-shelters (which had looked just like cages on the kitchen floor), until Morna had invented the zoo game. After that he had quite looked forward to sleeping in one of them with Morna during an air-raid, being a lion, a puma, or a tiger—or whatever Morna had decided they were to be that night.

3

He had also found it difficult to behave like a Newton when Miss Stearne, their governess, had raged at him. Quite often he might have burst into tears had it not been for Morna's fierce gaze daring him to disgrace her.

Morna had even managed to keep his nightmares secret. Gramarye was so deaf they had never woken her, and Bridget had slept downstairs at the back of the house, too far away to hear him.

"We're now in Suffolk," the knitting-lady announced. "Another fifteen minutes'll take us to Saxford."

"Good!" sighed Morna. "I'm tired of trains."

Nicholas did not look forward to the end of their journey with the same optimism for he was not particularly enthusiastic about staying with Aunt Dorothy. After all, he had been very happy at Gramarye's, living in the quiet, tree-lined avenue, being spoiled by Bridget and petted by Gramarye's friends, reading any book he wished from the study, playing Morna's wonderfully inventive games. Only Miss Stearne's daily visits had cast a slight shadow, but Morna had helped him cope even with those.

And now they were to live with a virtual stranger whom they had not seen since the day they had arrived in England from India. Morna said that Aunt Dorothy (who was their mother's sister) had taken them out to tea in a London hotel on that occasion, but Nicholas could not remember it at all. He and Morna had received regular gifts of birthday and Christmas money from Aunt Dorothy and her husband, Uncle Robin, during the past six years, but no visits because they had been engaged in important war work.

Suddenly a terrifying thought came to Nicholas.

"Morna!" he exclaimed in his 'panic' voice.

"Well?"

"How will we know it really is Aunt Dorothy?"

"What do you mean?"

"We don't know what she looks like! It could be someone pretending to be her . . . a kidnapper!"

"Oh, Nick . . . Honestly! Aunt Dorothy wrote to Bridget

4

saying she would be waiting for us at Saxford Station on Tuesday, June the 11th, at ten past four. Didn't she, now? You saw the letter."

"Someone else might have seen it. Someone in the post office."

"Bless his heart!" chuckled the woman, looking up from the sock she was knitting.

"He has such an imagination," exclaimed Morna. "It quite wears me out."

"Haven't you ever been to your Aunt Dorothy's before, then?" asked the woman.

Morna explained that Aunt Dorothy and Uncle Robin had only recently bought the cottage in Suffolk, since when Uncle Robin, who spoke Russian, had been called on to help with displaced persons in Germany.

"So your aunt's on her own. She'll be glad of your company, I dare say," the woman remarked.

"I dare say," Morna agreed confidently.

When the train finally drew in to Saxford station, groaning and whining as though sharing Nicholas's reluctance to stop there, Morna spotted Aunt Dorothy immediately. She was standing at the ticket barrier.

"There!" she said triumphantly to Nicholas. "She looks just like Mummy does in her photos, only a lot taller. There's no mistaking her."

Nicholas had to agree, as he took the small case Morna handed him from the luggage-rack. (The rest of their possessions had been sent on in advance in two large trunks.)

"I hope she likes children," he said nervously.

"She'll love you, bless your heart, bound to!" the knitting-lady burst out, starting up from her seat to give Nicholas a hard, farewell hug. Morna stuck her hand out quickly, before she was subjected to the same treatment. "Well, goodbye!" she said with dignity. "It's been very pleasant talking to you."

She always knew what to say and how to say it, Nicholas thought enviously. She was the sort of girl people looked at with approval while they remarked upon how pretty she was, or how clever, or how gracefully she moved. Whereas if anyone happened to give him a second glance, it was usually one of sympathy or of amusement because he had done something stupid.

"Go on!" he urged, pressing his legs hard against the seat so that Morna could pass him. "You go first." For he had just looked out of the window and seen Aunt Dorothy striding purposefully towards their compartment door.

2

First Impressions

Aunt Dorothy was all right. She had a cloud of frizzy, copper-coloured hair and when she smiled, which she did often, she showed a row of large, white, even teeth. As she led the way out of the station to her battered-looking Morris, Nicholas could see how straight-backed she walked, with a springy step, her hands thrust deep into the pockets of her white-spotted navy dress.

Yes, Nicholas decided. He liked Aunt Dorothy. He was too shy, however, to talk to her as Morna was doing, trotting along beside her, telling her about the journey, about Gramarye, even about Bridget and the liberty-bodice. Her long, dark plaits were swinging like pendulums in time to her brisk walk.

When they reached the car Morna slipped treacherously into the front passenger seat leaving Nicholas to creep alone into the back. He felt abandoned and suddenly queasy with home-sickness. Aunt Dorothy had not forgotten him, though.

"All right, Sir Nicholas?" she enquired in her light, pleasant voice, turning to give him a wink.

He felt better immediately and leaned forward to rest his arms on the back of Morna's seat so that he would not be left out of the conversation.

They turned right out of the small station yard and began to climb a winding hill.

"Look!" Morna cried. "Houses with thatched roofs and shutters, just like a story-book, Nick! And no pavements or lamp-posts anywhere! What do the dogs do? Use trees, I suppose."

Aunt Dorothy laughed, and Nicholas screwed his face up ferociously, as though trying to scare his short-sighted eyes into focussing properly. It was no good, though. The houses were too far away. He could see them, but they were blurred as though hiding behind a curtain of falling water.

The road levelled out, then swept round in a wide, right-hand bend. At the beginning of this bend, an unsurfaced track ran down to the left, between a long row of shabby cottages and, on the right, what looked like an oval-shaped potato field. (Nicholas recognized potato plants because Gramarye had grown them in her back garden.) Aunt Dorothy turned down this track, easing the car gently over unavoidable potholes and lumps of flint. She pointed out the village stores and the post office, the butcher's, and the Swan pub, all of which looked just like the other cottages, but with larger windows and swinging signs. The potato field, she told them, was really the village green which would be grassed over again once the country's food supplies were back to normal. At the bottom of the track they joined a metalled road and saw that there was another track running up the far side of the potato-field village green.

As they crossed a bridge and started to climb again they passed a large red-brick house on their left.

"That's the schoolhouse where Mr Grimes, the head teacher, lives," Aunt Dorothy told them. "We're just coming to the school. It's past four, though, so you won't see any of the children."

"Oh, look!" cried Morna, pointing to a poster on the playground wall. "It's another of those rat-notices. You must hear this, Aunt Dorothy! Do you know what Nick thought?"

But as Nicholas's shoulders hunched and his face began to

7

burn in anticipation of Morna's betrayal, Aunt Dorothy let out an exclamation and put her foot hard on the brake. She was looking into the schoolyard where some sort of battle was in progress. In a moment the two main protagonists came spilling out to roll like tumbleweed on to the road in front of the car.

Nicholas stood up, leaning forward as far as he could between Morna and Aunt Dorothy so that he could see what was happening. A large boy with cropped ginger hair, a brick-red face and glaring eyes was kneeling on top of a smaller boy whose face was invisible because he was hiding it with two dust-covered hands. The large boy's beefy fists hammered down rhythmically on the small boy's chest. Thump! Thump! Thump! Nicholas, who had never seen boys fighting in earnest before (though he had read about it in stories), felt his own heart begin to thump painfully in sympathy. He heard Morna make an excited, hissing sound through her teeth. Aunt Dorothy, having given a single, exasperated, "Tut!" sat still and silent, her hand on the door handle, as though she were awaiting a signal to leap out.

Thump! Thump! Thump! went the ugly fists as half-a-dozen yelling boys erupted through the school gate to form a ragged semicircle of spectators. They all looked as though they, too, had been rolling in the dust, with shirt sleeves pushed up high above grimy elbows and socks pushed down to bulge around their ankles. Their flushed, sweating faces contorted into hideous grimaces as they screamed at one another and at the two bodies on the ground. Suddenly the smallest of them darted forward to aim a kick at the boy who was being punched.

"That does it!" exclaimed Aunt Dorothy, and the car door flew open.

Nicholas watched admiringly as she hauled the boy with the flailing fists to his feet by the back of his collar, wagged an admonishing finger at the one with the flailing foot, and frowned fiercely at the others.

The boy on the ground uncovered his face, rolled over

8

twice, and sprang to his feet, racing off downhill like a whippet.

"How rude!" exclaimed Morna. "He didn't even thank her!"

Nicholas, however, was more concerned about the thug who had been robbed of his victim. What would he do now? Turn on Aunt Dorothy and butt her in the stomach? Summon his allies (for he certainly had some there) to attack the car? To his surprise and relief, however, the boy merely lowered his head and trudged disconsolately back into the playground with the other six shuffling along in his wake.

3

Home

"Well," began Morna with a bubbling little laugh as soon as Aunt Dorothy was settled in her seat again, "what was that all about?"

Nicholas could tell that she was excited, but he also knew that the fight had not upset or frightened her as it had him. Indeed he suspected from her voice that she might even have enjoyed it.

"It was about the Footers and the Buggs," Aunt Dorothy replied with a sigh as she started the engine. "Two village families who have some absurd, sixty-two-year-old feud. The little lad was Tommy Bugg, my daily help's boy, and the big one was Spikey Footer. Outsiders aren't supposed to interfere, but Mrs Bugg is a widow with plenty of other problems, so I feel I have to step in sometimes."

Nicholas was relieved to see that they were leaving the school and the village 'roughs' far behind. He tended to regard other children with mistrust at the best of times, probably because he had mixed with them so infrequently. Gramarye's friends had brought a grandchild or two along for a treat occasionally, but then they had been kept under the eye of the grown-ups in the drawing room. As for the few friends Morna had made during their daily outings to the park, they had never been encouraged to visit them in case, on closer acquaintance, they proved noisy or rough. "For once you open your door to people it's difficult to keep them out," Gramarye had declared, and Nicholas had felt that she was right. After all, hadn't he had to protect the fragile toy theatre on two occasions from Emily Russell, Mrs Rawlinson-Fox's grand-daughter, who looked as though butter wouldn't melt in her mouth? Oh, yes! He had always thought it much pleasanter when there had just been himself and Morna playing together.

"You live a long way from the village, Aunt Dorothy," he observed happily; for he had just looked back to discover that the school and the green were now quite hidden round a bend.

"It seems like it when I have a heavy load of shopping to carry," she remarked, adding, "I can only use the car on special occasions, of course, because of the petrol rationing."

"We can do the shopping for you now," said Morna kindly.

And immediately Nicholas began to worry. To reach the shops they would have to pass the school, so he did hope Aunt Dorothy would want her shopping done well inside school hours, and not at lunchtime or near four o'clock in the afternoon.

"I went shopping with Bridget every day," Morna rattled on. "So you can trust me with the ration-books, in case you were wondering about that. As a matter of fact I looked after the books for Bridget, because her eyes are very bad. And I'll queue for you, too, if you like, Aunt Dorothy. I can stand for a very long time, can't I, Nick? Once I stood for two hours for tomatoes, and they turned out to be horrid—like little green marbles."

"Well it's kind of you to offer," said Aunt Dorothy, "and I'll probably be glad of your help with the shopping. But we don't have queuing in the two village shops, thank goodness! Mrs Nelson at the Stores is very fair, even to a newcomer like me. I'd only been here a week when the first bananas came in, but I

10

had my allocation like everyone else."

"Bananas!" Morna started. "We haven't even seen one yet, Aunt Dorothy." Then her mouth closed and her eyes opened wide because the car was drawing to a halt outside a thatched house. On the white wooden gate was a sign on which *Elmtree Farm Cottage* had been painted.

"Is this it?" asked Nicholas, standing up. "Are we home?"

"We are," replied their aunt. "Do you like it?"

Morna was already out of the car and standing by the gate, clasping and unclasping her hands excitedly. "Come on, Nick! Hurry!" she called peremptorily. "Come and look!"

Nicholas shuffled along the seat and after a moment's delay, caused by a sticking door handle, joined her.

He could see immediately what he liked about the cottage. It was its determination to be private. It sat sideways to the road, the thatch of its high roof pulled low over narrow, arched windows like a wavy-brimmed hat. Best of all, its garden was enclosed by a high, thick privet hedge.

We can play in there and not a person will be able to see us, he thought with a great sense of comfort. Not that they seemed to have many neighbours, for the only building he could see was a misty, pink shape about two hundred yards further on along the road.

"That's Elmtree Farm," Aunt Dorothy told him, noticing the direction in which he was gazing. "That's where Mr Ward who sold us the cottage lives. I expect you'll want to pay him a visit soon to look at his animals. He has the fattest pigs I've ever seen."

"I shan't want to move an inch from this darling place!" Morna declared. "Will you, Nick?"

"No," he replied emphatically.

"To tell the truth," said Aunt Dorothy, whose mouth was twitching a little at the corners, "the outside's the best of it, my pets. Perhaps you'd better reserve your judgement until you've been on a conducted tour. Come along," she added, pushing open the gate. "We'll leave the car outside for the time being. Follow me."

11

Nicholas's first disappointment was the discovery that the piece of garden in front of the cottage (which ran for fifty yards or so behind the hedge) would be no playground after all; it was an enormous vegetable plot, crammed with regimented rows of beans, peas, onions and lettuces, and bisected by a narrow, gravelled path. There was someone in it, too. He could just make the figure out, moving around at the far end.

"That's Simon Bugg, keeping the weeds down for me," said Aunt Dorothy.

"He's not very friendly," remarked Morna. "He saw us. But he's pretending that he didn't."

"He's not well," Aunt Dorothy explained. "He's been in a Japanese prison camp, poor boy. He won't bother you, though."

She opened the front door of the cottage and led the way into a dark lobby. The door on the left was open to reveal the untidiest room Nicholas had ever seen. There were books and papers all over it; on the chairs and on the floor, as well as in mountainous heaps on the desk before the window.

"That's my study," Aunt Dorothy told them. "That's where I do my translations. When I lock myself away in there (which I do quite a lot) I mustn't be disturbed on any account."

The way she said this was not unpleasant. But for a moment she dropped her easy-going, friendly manner and showed that there was a straight-faced grown-up behind it who would not suffer annoyances gladly. All Nicholas's apprehension returned. What did they really know about Aunt Dorothy? Perhaps she didn't like children at all! After all, she had none of her own.

When he followed Morna into the living room on their right, his spirits sank even further; for after Gramarye's spacious rooms this one was like a broom cupboard. The ceiling was so low that, had Aunt Dorothy reached upwards, she could have touched it. The fireplace was no more than a hole in a plastered alcove, like a cave-mouth with bars across it. As for the table, chairs, and sideboard, they looked as though they had been engaged in some fierce war of their own, so disfigured were they by chips and scratches.

"We haven't been able to do anything to it yet, of course," Aunt Dorothy said apologetically. "It's just as we bought it, contents and all. Once wood and bricks are available again we'll have a new fireplace put in, and redecorate, and buy new furniture. Mind you," she went on more cheerfully, "it has its good points. Running water, for one. None of the village houses have that. They use wells. Mr Ward had it laid on to the farm and this cottage before the war. And they should be bringing us electricity next year. So we'll be rid of those smoky old oil lamps."

As they trooped through from the living room into the long kitchen, Nicholas tried hard to catch Morna's eye. Had she heard? Had she understood? No electricity! What would they do if he had one of his nightmares and there was no light to switch on? Would Aunt Dorothy allow them to have an oil lamp and matches in their room? Would they have to tell her about the nightmares? Morna obviously had not realized there was a problem, for she had run gaily to the other end of the kitchen to look at the copper, and was now dancing back, her shiny eyes darting everywhere, except in Nicholas's direction.

"What's that?" she asked, pointing to what looked like a massive, black iron sideboard with pots and a huge black kettle sitting on top of it.

Aunt Dorothy said it was an old-fashioned cooking range, and pulled down a flap in the centre to show them the red, glowing coals behind the bars.

"Mrs Bugg's the one who can handle this," she told them.

The kitchen was in one of the two annexes which, Aunt Dorothy said, had been added to the cottage forty years before, and which stuck out on either side of it like ears. The second annexe contained Aunt Dorothy's bedroom (leading off from her study) and behind it, the bathroom. The latter had two doors, one leading into Aunt Dorothy's bedroom, and the other into the back bedroom, which was to be Morna's and Nicholas's.

"Mademoiselle! Monsieur! Your quarters!" Aunt Dorothy

bowed from the waist as she ushered them through from the bathroom.

"Glory!" cried Morna, diving forward on to her bed where her Russian doll, Anastasia, was sitting. "All our things are waiting for us. Look, Nick!"

Sure enough, there was Nooka, the monkey with one ear, propped up on Nicholas's pillow on top of his pyjamas, and his zoo animals set out on the chest of drawers.

"Look in the wardrobe!" Aunt Dorothy called.

Nicholas opened the heavy oak door and there were Morna's dresses, skirts and coats on the left-hand side, and his own shirts and jackets on the right.

"Thank you very much, Aunt Dorothy," he said politely.

Suddenly he was much happier. Someone who did not like children would not have taken all this trouble to make them feel at home. Besides, it was a cheerful room. As well as having two doors (the other one led into the lobby) it had pretty wallpaper with bluebirds and nosegays of pink flowers, and a window seat. Morna, kneeling on this, called him to her side.

"Look!" she said. "An enormous orchard!"

"Yes," said Aunt Dorothy. "I should think you'll enjoy playing there. It has lovely long grass, good trees for climbing, and an old summerhouse at the far end. Can you see it?"

"Yes," said Morna.

"No," said Nicholas, screwing his eyes up in vain.

"Come on," said Aunt Dorothy, striding across the room and into the lobby. "Last port of call." She flung open the door opposite. "This will be another back bedroom one day," she told them. "At the moment it's full of junk. You can poke about here on wet days."

Nicholas looked at the rolls of carpet, the piles of old news-papers and the cartons overflowing with books, clothes, and exciting-looking bric-a-brac. "Gosh!" he exclaimed. "There's even a birdcage! Can we poke about now?"

"Oh, no!" protested Morna. "I'm dying of hunger!"

"Poor lambs!" said Aunt Dorothy remorsefully. "So you must be. Come on! Let's eat right away. I've a few more things to say to you, but I'll save them until tomorrow. You both look tired, and I expect you want to write a note to Gramarye after dinner."

"And to Mummy and Daddy," said Morna. "We write a little bit to them every evening and post it all off at the end of the week. And Mummy does the same for us."

As it turned out, though, Morna had to write both letters by herself for Nicholas fell fast asleep with a spoonful of junket halfway to his lips, and had to be carried off to bed and put into his pyjamas by Aunt Dorothy.

As soon as he woke next morning, Morna told him what he had done in her tightest, most scornful voice, making it plain that she was thoroughly ashamed of him for having behaved in such a babyish way.

4

Looking Around

"Well, I didn't have a nightmare, at any rate," Nicholas remarked cheerfully as he set out with Morna on Wednesday afternoon to explore the orchard.

They had both slept extraordinarily late, almost until midday, and then, since it was raining, they had spent an hour after lunch arranging their toys and books in the big cupboard in their room. Now, however, the sky had cleared and the sun was shining.

"A nightmare! I should think not!" Morna exclaimed. "That would have been too much! On top of the other thing, I mean."

"People can't help falling asleep," protested Nicholas.

"You looked so stupid!" said Morna. "I've never been so embarrassed in my life."

Nicholas was in too good a humour, though, to be upset by Morna's carping. For a start he was enjoying the novel experience of walking sockless and shoeless through long, wet grass. This had been Aunt Dorothy's suggestion when she had discovered that they did not own wellington boots. "It won't do you any harm," she had said. "And it will save your shoes and sandals. When you go round to the yard, of course, you'll have to cover your feet."

Nicholas was also savouring the rare pleasure of being able to see in sharp detail that normally misted world which lay outside his six-foot range of vision. This was Aunt Dorothy's doing. When she had learned at lunchtime that he owned spectacles, but hardly ever wore them because Gramarye, Bridget, and Morna thought they spoiled his appearance, she had looked disbelieving at first, then mildly angry.

'Well, I think it's very silly," she had declared finally, patting Nicholas's hand. "Poor Nicholas is missing out on a lot of enjoyment for other people's benefit. After all I don't suppose he sits all day in front of a mirror telling himself how handsome he looks!"

"No! I do not!" Nicholas burst out, his face burning.

"In any case," she went on, "I expect his spectacles suit him quite well. It's just a question of other people becoming used to them."

"Shall I begin wearing them today, then?" Nicholas had asked, aware that Morna's head was drooping sulkily because she disapproved.

"Yes. I think you should," Aunt Dorothy had told him, and he had rushed off to root them out from the bottom of his small suitcase.

Now he could see even the holes in the thatch of the distant summerhouse roof, and a tiny, singing bird suspended in the air above the wheat field on the other side of the hedge. He felt very happy all of a sudden, and he wanted to share his happiness with Morna. How could he please her? He looked round at the tall apple trees rising from a rippling sea of grass. Then his eye fell on the summerhouse again and an idea began to unfold in his head. The grass was a southern ocean, the trees tall ships, the summerhouse a hut on a deserted island. Morna should be Robinson Crusoe, and he her Man Friday!

He gripped Morna's arm. In his eagerness to tell her what he had dreamed up, the words spilled out of him, tripping over one another.

"All right!" she said, frowning. "Don't get so excited. We can't possibly start playing games until we've explored the place properly. You surely didn't expect us to!"

Nicholas supposed Morna was right although, secretly, he thought that—with so many days stretching ahead of them— they might have spared this afternoon for the Robinson Crusoe game. They probably would have done so had Morna invented it, he reflected sourly.

They walked down to inspect the summerhouse which was in fact rather disappointing, since it contained nothing but a semicircular bench, the ends of which had rotted away. Then they went back to collect their sandals from the kitchen door so that they could walk round to the yard and outhouses. As Nicholas straightened, after fastening his sandals, he happened to look through the narrow window beside the door. He saw that there was now a stranger in the kitchen—a thin, worried-looking little woman with her hair scraped up beneath a floral turban and a cigarette drooping from the corner of her mouth. She had piled the rugs up in a corner and was sweeping the brick floor energetically with a hard brush.

It must be Mrs Bugg, he thought, but he decided not to tell Morna in case she insisted they go in to introduce themselves.

He let Morna lead the way round to the cobbled yard, her grey kilt swinging jauntily against her long, white legs. Once there, she marched straight for the outhouses, two low red-brick buildings with tiled roofs. The outhouse nearer the orchard was open-fronted and divided by a brick partition into two equal-sized compartments. In the left-hand one Aunt Dorothy's car was sitting. The other was empty (or appeared to be).

"And now! What have we here?" asked Morna, her voice sharpening with curiosity as they moved along to the neigh-bouring, longer building. It had two closed doors: one of

17

normal width at the end nearer to Aunt Dorothy's car; and a much wider one at the other end. There was a small, barred window, set high up in the wall to the left of each door.

"It might once have been some kind of animal feeding-house," suggested Nicholas cautiously. "Perhaps the animals went in through the ordinary door, and after they'd eaten, they were so fat they needed a specially wide door to go out by."

As he finished speaking, Morna's head whipped round and her eyes widened. She walked forward so that she was standing very close to him.

"Someone laughed just then," she whispered, bending her head so that her mouth was against his ear. "Didn't you hear?"

He shook his head. But a moment later he did hear. It was a stifled, sniggering, sobbing sort of sound, but unmistakeably laughter.

"Let's run away, Morna," he murmured shakily.

"No!" Morna whispered fiercely. "That wouldn't be behaving like a Newton!"

She drew herself up, took a deep breath, then called loudly, "We know you're there, whoever you are! So you'd just better come out and show yourself!" An unspoken *or else!* trailed after her words to hang threateningly over the yard. How did she dare, marvelled Nicholas. Anyone might appear! The queer man who worked in the vegetable plot, for example.

"Did you hear me?" shouted Morna, injecting a little more menace into her tone.

There was a sudden scuffle behind Nicholas and, as he whirled round in alarm, a rough voice said crossly, "Hold hard there! No need to git all windy. I were only havin' a bit of a giggle at what the little old fellow said!"

18

5

Buggs

A girl walked slowly out of the open-fronted outhouse from the compartment they had thought was empty. She was about Morna's height but had such a mass of curly, straw-coloured hair that she looked oddly top-heavy. From beneath it her sharp blue eyes met and locked with Morna's gleaming dark ones. Nicholas, ignored by them both, moved aside and waited nervously for the outcome of the confrontation.

"What were you doing in there?" Morna demanded. "Do you know our Aunt Dorothy?"

"Mrs Buchanan?" said the girl scornfully. "I should do, shouldn't I, since my Mam does for her? I'm Louie Bugg," she finished in a tone that implied that Morna must surely have heard of her.

To Nicholas's surprise, his sister descended with unusual rapidity from her high-horse, obviously realizing that in Louie Bugg she had met her match. She began to tell her their names, but it was clear that Louie knew these already; and not only their names, but their ages, and most of their past history.

"Mam reckons its real hard on you bein' sent to this old neck of the woods after town-dwellin' with electricity an' that," Louie said, including Nicholas in a sudden friendly smile.

"Oh, we like it much better here," Morna assured her, adding, with a shocking disloyalty that made Nicholas blush for her, "I mean it wasn't much fun living with an old fusspot like Bridget."

Before Nicholas quite realized what was happening, Morna and Louie had linked arms, and Louie was opening the doors of the long outhouse, explaining that it was really two buildings under the same roof: a cowhouse and a stable. The narrower door led to the old cowhouse, now occupied by a thriving mushroom-bed, while the stable at the other end was used to store everything from apples to paraffin.

19

The two girls, laughing and talking, began to saunter across the yard towards the front of the cottage with Nicholas trailing awkwardly behind. He could see that if he did not soon remind them of his presence, he was in danger of being totally forgotten. He wracked his brains for something to say to Louie. Finally in desperation he tapped her on the shoulder to ask abruptly, "Why aren't you at school this afternoon?"

As soon as the words were out he knew he had sounded like a policeman, so it was no surprise to him when Louie swung round and replied rudely, "Rats!" Nicholas looked towards Morna to see whether she was going to help him out of this particular sticky situation. Then he realized that Louie was chatting on quite blithely. "School's swarmin' with the little old blighters," she was saying. "One jumped clean out of the piano yesterday mornin' when old Grim-fizz (that's Mr Grimes, the headmaster) was playin' the marchin' hymn. Should've seen 'is face! Should've seen us gels! Up on top of the desks screamin' blue murder! So some Council blokes've turned up this arternoon an' they've give us the rest of the day off. Reckon it'll take more 'an one arternoon to cetch them little old varmints, though!"

"We've never seen a real, live rat," Nicholas observed, relieved that he had not, after all, put Louie's back up. He quickened his pace so that he was level with the two girls. Oddly enough, this second remark had a more dramatic effect on Louie than his previous one. She stopped and her blue eyes glared at him disbelievingly.

"Corblast!" she exclaimed after a moment. "Never seen a real, live rat! Blast! Can't hardly believe that!"

"It's true," said Nicholas stoutly. "Isn't it true, Morna?"

"Of course I've seen rats," said Morna, tight-lipped. "I've seen rats out in India."

It was Morna's dirtiest trick to pretend to have done or seen things in India because, although Nicholas knew very well her stories were untrue, he could not disprove them. He stuck his tongue out at her behind Louie's back and saw her redden with anger.

Then an unnerving, high wail, reminiscent of an air-raid siren, came floating over between the cottage chimneys, and Louie gripped their arms, not in alarm, but in exultation. "That's Mam!" she cried. "Come you on, together! Beevers!"

She began to drag them back round the corner of the cottage and across the yard. As Nicholas trotted along by her side his heart was pounding. He knew about beavers, because he had read about them in Gramarye's encyclopedia. He had not realized there were any still living in England, though. There must surely be a river nearby! Were they going to watch them? he wondered. Or feed them? Or chase them away, like the boy who chased donkeys for Betsy Trotwood in *David Copperfield?*

When they arrived at the kitchen door, however, the only animal to be seen was a thin orange cat which, Louie said, belonged to Mr Ward, the farmer. She barred its way with her foot while she pushed Morna and Nicholas into the kitchen ahead of her.

"Hello, my old darlins! Come for beevers, hev you? Made friends with my Louie, hev you? Set you down, then!" Mrs Bugg greeted them in a purring, velvety voice that did not seem to fit in with the rest of her at all. "Your auntie said as I was to look out for you mid-arternoon to give you a bite to eat, like," she went on. "She's a-settin' in that old study-room, poor old gel, darned near buried under papers."

Mrs Bugg turned back to the range, and Nicholas and Morna sat down dumbly on the two seats to which they had been directed by her waggling finger. Nicholas's stomach was already turning somersaults at the very idea of eating beaver. He couldn't. He just couldn't! He had never been able to bring himself to eat rabbit even, despite Gramarye's and Bridget's coaxing. He glanced at Morna who was staring stonily at the wall. He could not guess what she was thinking. There was no help there. I shall just say I'm not hungry, he decided. They can't force me to eat. (In the 'they' he was including Louie who darted back and forth between the dresser and the table, laying out cups and plates, and making a humming noise like a musical saw.)

21

Suddenly two large plates descended on the table. One held rusks, spread thinly with margarine and grated cheese; the other wheaten biscuits sandwiched together with jam.

"Eat you up, together!" Mrs Bugg said encouragingly. "Kettle's now a-boilin' for tea."

Nicholas looked hard at Louie who had just taken her seat opposite him, then at the back of Mrs Bugg who was pouring water from the large black kettle into an equally large brown teapot. Were they a couple of practical jokers?

"Where are the beavers then?" he asked abruptly, in a much louder voice than his normal one, because he had had to overcome his shyness to force it out. "I can't see any."

"Blast!" exclaimed Louie, staring at him as though he were mad. "What's that a-settin' in front of you?"

Nicholas looked down at the table. "Afternoon tea," he replied after a moment.

"What!" Louie covered her face and began to make the sobbing, snorting noise they had heard in the outhouse.

"Shut you up, Louie Bugg!" ordered her mother sharply. "A-showin' your ignorance! That's what it is, true enough, my little old love," she said kindly to Nicholas. "Arternoon-tea. 'Beevers' is jes' our countryfied way of sayin' it."

"Anyone would have guessed that," put in Morna, throwing Nicholas a flinty look.

The door opened suddenly and a gaunt, frizzy-haired young man in overalls came in. He strode the length of the kitchen in silence, passing behind Nicholas to sit down on a chair by the sink. Immediately Mrs Bugg piled a small plate with rusks and biscuits and poured out a cup of tea.

"Do you take those over to your brother, Louie," Nicholas heard her whisper, and he saw her pale eyes which were naturally watery grow suddenly brighter and moister. By the time Louie had returned to the table, Simon Bugg, crouched over his food and eating ravenously, had half-cleared his plate. A few minutes later he rose and went out again as silently as he had come in.

"Poor old lad!" Mrs Bugg burst out as soon as the door had

closed behind him. "He don't mean to be rude. Jes' can't bring himself to say a word, not even to his nearest an' dearest. Fares like he's been struck dumb, all the horrors he's saw!"

"Don't you go upsettin' yerself again over Simon, Mam," said Louie, shoving the plate of rusks invitingly towards Nicholas. "That won't do no good. It's our Tommy we should be a-wurritin' about. Real little roughneck he's a-gittin' to be. Fightin' Footers! Fares he an' Cousin Charlie can't think on nothin' else these days."

"Where is he, anyways?" asked Mrs Bugg, sitting down. She put her elbows on the table and hunched her shoulders, her brow corrugated with worry. Nicholas thought she looked like an anxious tortoise about to withdraw into its shell.

"Up the woods with Charlie," said Louie. "Fetchin' sticks."

"Well, that's doin' no harm," Mrs Bugg pointed out. "I'm wantin' sticks as a matter of fac'. Dratted old stove fare to eat them. It truly do!"

"Footers is up the wood, too," said Louie.

"Which?"

"Spikey. Georgie. Monty. Big Mary."

Mrs Bugg gave a deep sigh, then remained silent for so long that Nicholas—who did not like to peer at her—wondered whether she had dozed off. Suddenly, though, she raised her head and said resolutely, "Louie! Run you along an' fetch Tommy back home."

"Oh, Mam!" protested Louie in a foghorn-like bleat. "I'm a-showin' these two round!"

"These two!" repeated Mrs Bugg. "Where's your manners, gel, that you can't call folks by their given names? Anyways, I reckon Morna an' Nicholas don't need no showin' round, them comin' from the city an' all! Reckon they can look arter themselves!"

Nicholas, seeing his chance to be rid of Louie, immediately slid from his chair and said loudly, "Thank you very much for the tea, Mrs Bugg. It was lovely. Please may we leave the table now and go out to play?"

"Course you can, my old loves!" crooned Mrs Bugg,

23

obviously impressed by this display of good manners. "Run you along now."

Morna was forced to rise too, murmur her thanks, and follow Nicholas with a regretful look back at her new friend.

"Well!" she started angrily as soon as they were clear of the back door.

But Nicholas was already several yards ahead of her and making for the front of the cottage.

"Where are you going?" she called.

"Along the road to look at the farm," he replied, without stopping.

She hurried to catch up with him, as he had known she would, and by the time they arrived, breathless, at the gate of Elmtree Farm she had forgotten all about Louie Bugg.

6

Abraham and Amos

By the end of a week Nicholas had not had a single nightmare, and he felt that he had always lived in small rooms with shabby furniture and oil lamps. To his surprise life in the cottage was much pleasanter than he had expected. For a start there was no need to worry about damaging furniture accidentally. (At Gramarye's he and Morna had always had to be careful not to kick the chair legs or to mark the polished tables by leaning too heavily on their pencils.) The smallness of the living room seemed no longer cramping but cosy, and he loved to sit there with Morna and listen to Aunt Dorothy telling them stories before they went to bed about when she and their mother were children.

Aunt Dorothy worked in her study for most of each day and left them to Mrs Bugg and their own devices. She had given them a little talk on the day after their arrival about what they must and must not do. Mostly this was to do with what she

24

called the countryside code and was a matter of common sense: she said she was sure they had plenty. They were not to walk on crops. They had to close farm gates behind them. They were never to start fires, break branches from trees, or interfere with farm machinery. ("As though we ever would!" Morna had whispered indignantly to Nicholas.)

The other code they had to follow was the bread code, which was pinned up in the kitchen, and was about not wasting a single crumb of bread. It applied to all food, of course, Aunt Dorothy said. And she told them how the poor people Uncle Robin was working with were very nearly dying of hunger; and that a friend of hers who worked in Whitehall had told her that bread was likely to be rationed soon, which it had never been during the war.

Basically, though, Aunt Dorothy was a free and easy person who said that she did not believe in young people being fenced around by rules and regulations. So they were allowed to carry on in a way that would have made Bridget and Gramarye exclaim in horror. They wore what they wanted. They ate out of doors whenever they wished. Once they had even splashed through the heavy dew in the orchard to eat their breakfast cereal in the summerhouse. (This had not been a great success, though, since the seat had been uncomfortably damp under their pyjama'd behinds, and the floor had been thick with nocturnal creepy-crawlies on their belated way home.) They frequently wandered up to the farm to watch the haymaking or to look at the pigs and the horses. And they explored the village.

It was Morna, of course, who always wanted to go further afield. Nicholas would have amused himself quite happily in the vicinity of the cottage. Morna, however, had taken over Aunt Dorothy's shopping and was now on polite, chatting terms with Mrs Nelson at the Stores and Mr Vout, the butcher. She loved the daily trips to the shops, and soon she was marching Nicholas to the far end of the village to prowl round the churchyard, where they read the mossy ghosts of inscriptions on the staggery old stones. She coaxed him up shadowy twists of lanes between cottages to find hidden meadows, like green lakes, where cream-and-auburn cows stood dreamily tail-swinging. Once she trailed him reluctantly along a flint-strewn track which was signposted, 'To The Camp'; and at the end of it they found family-washing strung up and babies crawling around what looked like army huts. Most astounding of all, they spotted Mrs Bugg dismounting from her big, old bicycle and disappearing into one of the huts!

When they mentioned this later to Aunt Dorothy, she explained that Mrs Bugg had moved her family to the disused army camp out of a very ramshackle old cottage so that she would be high on the list for one of the new council houses that were soon to be built in the village. The Buggs and the other families who had done the same were known as 'squatters', she said.

On all of these expeditions in and around the village Nicholas was always careful to see that they hurried past the school. He had a dread of any of the rough bunch spotting them from a window and marking them down as potential game. He was also afraid that old Grim-fizz might come running out to haul them off into a classroom. It was Mrs Bugg who had made him nervous on this score by remarking out of the blue one afternoon, "Ever so perticlar they are about schoolin' in Saxford! Wouldn't surprise me if the old attendance-man weren't up here arter you two soon!"

Aunt Dorothy had laughed when they had repeated this to her, and had said that the attendance-man was too busy tracking down the natives to worry about a couple of young holidaymakers. Still, it had left Nicholas uneasy.

Mrs Bugg never lost a chance of a chat with them. She said it cheered her up as Morna was a titbit and Nicholas a little old love. It was during one of these chats, on their second Tuesday afternoon in Saxford, that she told them the story of Abraham and Amos. They were enjoying their 'beevers', Aunt Dorothy having shut herself away in her study, and Simon having already slipped silently in and out like a grey, ravenous wolf.

Mrs Bugg was bemoaning the fact that Tommy had once again torn his trousers fighting Footers.

"Why must they always be fighting one another?" Morna asked, frowning. "How did it all start?"

"Why, that all started the day of the earthquake, my darlin'," Mrs Bugg replied, setting one elbow firmly on the table and waggling her cigarette.

"Earthquake? Here?" Nicholas wondered whether he had misheard.

"That's right," Mrs Bugg went on. "Wholly frightenin' that must've bin! The sky turnin' black an' the wind howlin'. Then them teeterin' old cottages a-tumblin' down. An' the church tower a-crackin'. An' them old bells jingle-janglin'. An' the ground heavin' up an' down like sea waves . . . There's plenty in the village still minds of it. That were in 1884, I believe. The Great Earthquake they called that."

"Was anyone killed?" asked Morna.

"One," replied Mrs Bugg. "An' that were one too many! That were Amos Bugg."

"I'm very sorry," Nicholas said politely, knowing that this was the drill when someone told you that a relative had died.

"So should we all be," remarked Mrs Bugg, stubbing her cigarette out energetically in her saucer. "For that were the start of it all, my old love. The feud atween Footers and Buggs, I mean." She clasped her red, stubby fingers together and leaned over the table towards Morna and Nicholas. "This is how it come about," she began. "There were this here Sick Club in the village. Poor folks paid a few coppers into that every week, like. An' happen they fell ill an' couldn't work, the Club give 'em money, so's they needn't go in the Workhouse. Well, on this day, the day of the earthquake, it were Amos Bugg and Abraham Footer what were carryin' that old Club money-box to the Swan for the weekly pay-out. It'd bin locked up safe in Amos's cottage, you see, an' the two of them were bringin' it over together, case of thieves or highwaymen . . ."

27

"I don't think there were highwaymen in 1884, Mrs Bugg," Morna put in diffidently.

"Well, whatever!" Mrs Bugg went on. "Anyways, they were a-comin' through what's now called Amos's Grove (that tiddy bit of wood at the foot of the hill. You can see it from the bottom of your auntie's orchard . . .). Then of course, before the trees were planted, that were jest an up-an-down bit o' common. They was there when the earthquake come at any rate. For arter it were over, they foun' poor old Amos dead as mutton on the ground, an' that Abraham Footer gone off with the Club money. The Buggs swore blin' Abraham'd killed Amos, though there weren't a mark on him. No one never saw Abraham again. An' from that day to this the Footers an' the Buggs've bin scrabblin' at one another's throats."

Mrs Buggs choked on a sigh as she finished, so that it came out like a sob, and for a moment Nicholas thought that she had been overcome by the sadness of her own story. He was relieved when she suddenly stood up, began to gather the dirty cups and plates, and said cheerfully, "Run you off into the sunshine, then! See if you can't git some colour into those little old faces!"

As soon as they were outside, Morna turned to Nicholas with kindling eyes. "Shall we go there?" she whispered. "To the scene of the crime? To where Amos Bugg received his mortal wound?"

"Mrs Bugg said he didn't have a wound," objected Nicholas.

"Stop being contrary," said Morna, reverting to her normal, sharp tone. "Do you want to go there or don't you?"

"Couldn't we just stay in the orchard and play at being Amos and Abraham?" Nicholas asked.

Morna, tossing her plaits disdainfully, was about to say what she thought of this suggestion when Louie Bugg suddenly came racing in from the road. She stood between them, clutching at her side and breathing like a steam-engine for several minutes. There was a look on her face, though, that suggested that she had just heard some good news.

"D'you know what?" she gasped, as soon as she had dredged up breath enough to speak. "Them Council blokes've come again 'bout the rats. An' now they've had old Grim-fizz shut the school up till September! Mus' tell Mam!" she finished, and vanished into the kitchen.

"Come on, then, Morna!" said Nicholas hastily. "If you want to see that place, let's go."

Louie was too quick for him, though. Her dandelion-clock head poked out of the door even as he finished speaking. "Mam says I can play," she announced.

"Oh, good!" said Morna gushingly. "We want to see Amos's Grove. Can you take us there?"

"Course I can," replied Louie, closing the door behind her with a triumphant bang. "Come along, little 'un!" she called to Nicholas as she grabbed Morna's arm and set off down the orchard.

"He look like a little old owl in those specs, don't he?" Nicholas heard her remark to Morna as he caught up with them.

7

Fightin' Footers

Having climbed the fence at the bottom of the orchard Louie, Morna and Nicholas turned left to walk in Indian file along the path that bordered the wheat field. Invisible larks sang, and whenever the breeze rippled the green wheat it looked as though the whole field were moving to the music.

Had he been on his own with Morna, Nicholas would have told her his thoughts about the singing sky and the dancing field. As it was, Morna was engaged in a loud, shouting conversation with Louie, the latter tossing remarks over her shoulder without looking round while Morna lobbed back replies. It was stupid girls' talk, too, Nicholas noted with disgust, about scraps and paper-dolls, and Louie's sister, Maureen, who was a GI bride and lived in California.

Eventually they arrived at the far side of the field, where a deep ditch and then a tall, broad, springy-looking hedge separated wheat from woodland. Louie led them to a spot where there was a hole like a cave-mouth in the foot of the hedge. She sprang across the ditch, flung herself flat, then disappeared.

"Come you on, together!" her voice called encouragingly from behind the wall of foliage.

Morna jumped over and wriggled agilely after her.

Nicholas took a deep breath. Suddenly the ditch looked very wide. He leaped but, faltering at the last moment, missed his footing and slithered to the bottom. Before he could scrabble up again, Morna's scowling face loomed over him, and her hands reached down to grip his arms just above the elbows.

"Why did you do that?" she whispered fiercely. "Louie'll think you're stupid!"

"I couldn't help slipping . . ." he began. Then his nose hit the ground as Morna started to slide backwards into the hedge, hauling him up as she went. He realized that Louie must be at the end of the chain pulling Morna by the legs.

"I'm all right, now! Leave me alone! You'll break my glasses," he cried as he was dragged, head first, into the hole, his knees already barked and stinging. His arms were released and he crawled through to find the two girls standing waiting for him, Morna's eyes glinting with irritation, Louie's with amusement.

"Poor little old owl!" said Louie. "He look real ruffled!" Morna mouthed "Stupid!" at him, and he slid his foot over and trod hard on her little toe.

"That weren't very kind to your sister what's so good to you!" Louie said reprovingly, and Nicholas felt that the girls were ganging up against him, and that it was not fair, since all he had done was to fall accidentally into a ditch.

When they moved off along the spongey, shaded path Nicholas kept his distance behind the other two, stuck his fists

30

into his pockets, and whistled tunelessly. As Morna's high laugh rang out in response to something Louie had said, Nicholas made a face at her back. Girls! Why couldn't he have had a brother instead of a sister? The two of them could have shared interesting hobbies like bird-spotting, fishing, or stamp-collecting. He would have liked a brother called Victor. Victor Newton! It sounded cheerful and dependable. Vic for short, of course . . . He saw himself standing on a river bank struggling with an enormous fish and calling for his brother to help him: "Vi-i-c! Vi-i-c!"

"Ni-i-ck!" Morna exclaimed crossly as he walked full tilt into her. The path had been sloping gently downhill for quite some time and, without his noticing, Louie had halted just where it levelled out.

"Well," said Louie grandly, waving a hand towards the wooded incline on their right, "this here is Amos's Grove, where poor old Amos Bugg were murdered by wicked old Abraham Footer. They reckon it's haunted an' all."

"Do they?" Morna murmured with a faint smile.

Nicholas could tell that she was disappointed. After all there was nothing to see but an old tangle of thorny bushes with some taller trees poking up behind.

"I suppose we might as well go back now," she added flatly.

"Can't do nothin' else." Louie grinned, pointing to the track ahead where a five-barred gate blocked their way.

Nicholas walked up to the gate which had trimmings of barbed-wire dangling from it and three notices fixed down its centre. In descending order these read: *Danger, Keep Out, Prohibited Area*. He could see now that there was a barbed-wire fence running up the slope from the right-hand gatepost.

"Of course," said Louie, sauntering up with Morna to sneer at the gate, "that's really a load of old squit! That's only old Colonel Cutworth's Home Guard Bunker in there. That were never used hardly. D'you know why? Silly old codger built that right in at the foot of the hill. An' when that rained that were whoolly flooded out! *Colonel Duckworth* they called 'im arter that in the village."

31

"Can't we go in and look at it?" Nicholas asked.

"Not when that say, 'Keep Out'," Louie told him sternly. "Do you do that, old Cutworth'd be a-stickin' up *Passers Persecuted* notices all over the show. An' then where'd we be when Mam wanted firewood?"

"Don't you mean 'prosecuted'? Trespassers *prosecuted*?" Morna suggested with gentle tact.

"May be," said Louie non-committally. "Makes no odds how you say that, I reckon, if your old head git chopped off jes' the same."

Both Nicholas and Morna were laughing heartily at this joke until they realized from Louie's startled expression that she had been in earnest. Luckily they were saved the embarrassment of explanations by a sudden, faraway explosion of noise.

"People shouting!" exclaimed Morna, staring at Louie.

Louie listened, cocking her head from side to side like a bird tracking a worm. Finally she pinned the noise down. "Tommy an' Cousin Charlie fightin' Footers!" she declared. "Round at Keeper's Gallows. That's where they was a-headin' this arternoon! Reckon I'd better git along there to see if the little un's all right . . . Jes' you two follow the path back to the hole where we come in," she finished hastily as she started running.

"Hold on!" Morna cried. "We'll come with you, Louie! Won't you need some help?"

"Might do," admitted Louie. "Come you on, then!"

She started back the way they had come, with Morna hard on her heels. Nicholas, with his shorter legs, had difficulty in keeping up with them. Uphill and downhill they raced; along narrow, mossy tracks where branches caught at their clothes and sprang back in their faces; through cool, twilit glades where tall trees stood like pillars.

Louie had no need to tell them when they were approaching the battle-ground. As they slithered down a steep, mossy path the wave of shouting, screaming, and hurled insults rolled up to meet them.

I don't want to go on, thought Nicholas, stopping suddenly

32

as he spied the brightness of a clearing ahead. It will be that rough bunch from the village, and I don't want to go near them! Why should I?

At that moment Morna looked over her shoulder to make sure that he was coming, and signalled to him to hurry. Reluctantly he slithered on.

When he reached the clearing it was just as unpleasant as he had expected. There were six, yelling boys who seemed to be alternately rolling over on the grass and jumping on one another's backs. He watched Louie dive into the melee to grab Tommy, who looked as grimy and dishevelled as he had when Aunt Dorothy rescued him from Spikey Footer. As Louie pushed him none too gently ahead of her, he turned back to hurl a last insult. Immediately a head and neck reared up from a knot of bodies squirming on the grass and a bellowing Spikey came charging across the clearing to butt Louie in the back. As she fell forward with a surprised croak, Spikey aimed a kick at Tommy's behind.

It was then that, to Nicholas's dismay, Morna decided to enter the fray. As he saw her leaping forward, his heart contracted. She would be killed, or at least knocked senseless! He need not have worried. Before he could blink she had grabbed Spikey's plimsolled foot and toppled him over backwards. Then she sat on his chest.

The speed of Morna's manoeuvre, and the sureness with which she had carried it out, left everyone gaping. The Bugg-faction set up an instant cawing which Nicholas realized was cheering. Morna grinned, while Spikey threshed his arms and legs about foolishly and futilely.

Nicholas felt himself swell with pride. It was his sister who had saved the day for the Buggs! "Good old Morna!" he cried shrilly from his ringside stance. "Give him it!"

Immediately someone began to throttle him. An arm had whipped round his neck and was pressing against his windpipe in an effort to pull him to the ground. Then there was a yell and a scuffle behind him. The arm relaxed its grip. Nicholas wheeled, gasping, to find Tommy Bugg on the back of his assailant, a fat-faced boy with ginger Footer hair, which Tommy seemed bent on yanking out by the roots.

"Don't jes' stand there! Help me git 'im down!" Tommy bawled to Nicholas.

"No," Nicholas called shakily. "My glasses might get broken."

He turned away and hurried up the path to where a low-spreading bush offered both shelter and a vantage point. He crawled under this to watch the final stage of the hostilities. The difficulty seemed to lie in persuading Spikey Footer to admit that he was beaten, despite the fact that Morna still sat on his chest, Louie on his legs, and another Bugg (a skinny boy with protruding ears) held his arms. Gradually the other combatants ceased to fight. Even Tommy Bugg and the Throttler had exhausted themselves and went staggering over to the central group. Spikey groaned, and his pinioned limbs made convulsive movements, as though the very idea of submitting were agony to him. Then, just when it seemed they would be there all day, he roared, "Give in! Give in!"

Spikey's captors sprang aside as the big boy struggled to his feet. Nicholas thought he looked like a red-faced gorilla with his brows drawn down and his lips jutting out, humiliation making his shoulders droop. With racing heart Nicholas waited for some act of treachery. Spikey abided by the rules, though. With a wave of his arm he collected his followers and they trudged off up the path past Nicholas's bush. As they walked by he could hear them discussing in low voices what had gone wrong.

The four Buggs were dancing around Morna chanting exuberantly when Nicholas finally ran down to join them.

"V for victory, dot, dot dash,
Footer's lost his old moustache.
Spikey wore it, Morna tore it,
V for victory, dot, dot, dash!" they yelled in unison.

What a stupid rhyme! thought Nicholas. It doesn't make sense. He stood at the side, feeling awkward. Then Tommy Bugg spotted him.

"Here come little old Four-eyes at las'," he jeered. "Crawled out from under 'is bush. Couldn't fight case 'is glasses got broke!" The rest fell silent and stared at Nicholas.

A crimson tide surged over Morna's face. "You didn't say that, did you, Nick?" she asked sharply.

"Yes," he said, adding, "I'm sure I wouldn't enjoy fighting anyway, Morna. I only like the pretend-fighting we have in our games."

The boy with the protruding ears sniggered into his sleeve, and Morna looked down at her feet, chewing on her underlip. Even her ears were red now, Nicholas noted.

"Poor little old owl!" said Louie suddenly. "Don't you laugh at 'im, Charlie! He's only a little 'un, arter all!"

"He's older nor me! An' he's older nor Winston there!" Tommy pointed out querulously. "Mam says he's nine!"

"Shut you up, an' git you along home!" Louie snapped, giving him a shove. "An' we're a-goin' to see Aunt Connie this evenin'. So you'd bes' git tidied up!"

Tommy, Charlie, and Winston went scuttling off up the track, followed by Morna and Louie, with Nicholas bringing up the rear. Morna was talking animatedly to Louie, and Nicholas could hear phrases like 'plan of campaign', and 'lying in ambush' which suggested she was planning one of her games. He hoped it was either 'Robin Hood' or 'Hereward the Wake' which were his favourites.

They parted from Louie and her contingent at the hole in the hedge (for the Buggs left the woods by another exit nearer to the village) and Nicholas cleared the ditch splendidly this time. Morna made no comment, however, but strode off along the wheat-field path without a backward glance. Nicholas had to run to catch up with her.

"Morna!" he panted at her shoulder. "Were you planning out a game? Is that what you were talking to Louie about?"

She stopped, turning to frown at him. "If you must know," she said icily, "we were talking about fighting the Footers again tomorrow. But you're not much good at that sort of thing, are you?"

35

"No," Nicholas agreed meekly.

"So there's no point in telling you about it," she observed.

"Why not?" he demanded, trying to hide the fact that his feelings were hurt. Morna and he never had secrets from each other.

"Well, you won't be coming with us. Will you?" she asked.

Suddenly Nicholas sensed that, despite her manner, Morna was desperately anxious for him to say that he wanted to go with her to fight the Footers tomorrow, and to prove to her that he was a true Newton after all. At the same time he was aware of a new sensation inside him—a hard, uncomfortable, lumpy sort of feeling which made him say crossly, "No! I won't be coming, thank you!"

"Thank *you!*" retorted Morna, treating him to a final basilisk glare, before she set off again along the path with long, angry strides.

8

War in the Air

That evening they went to the 'War On Rats' exhibition in the village hall.

"I couldn't wriggle out of it," Aunt Dorothy told them apologetically at teatime. "Mr Grimes walked all the way up here in that broiling sun to ask me if I would take you two along to see it. The poor man has rats on the brain, I think. He talked about them non-stop for half-an-hour. Did you know that there wasn't a brown rat in Britain until after 1700? And that one female rat can produce ninety babies in a year?"

"I know nothing about rats. I've never even seen one," Nicholas replied.

"I expect you will before you've left Saxford," said Aunt Dorothy, laughing.

"Well, I hope Nick won't wear those awful specs when we

36

go down to the exhibition," Morna piped up suddenly, having remained remarkably silent up till then.

"Why ever not?" asked Aunt Dorothy indignantly. "And anyway they're not 'awful specs', silly girl! He looks very nice in them."

"People call him 'owl' and 'four-eyes'," Morna explained, her colour rising. She was not used to being addressed as 'silly girl'.

"I don't care what people call me," said Nicholas, aware of that uncomfortable, hard knot tightening inside him again. "I'm not going to stop wearing my glasses."

"I should think not!" said Aunt Dorothy.

Later, however, as he trailed around the exhibition with his tight-lipped, sulky sister carefully keeping half the room between them, Nicholas wondered whether it might not have been easier to have given in to Morna about the spectacles. Just before they had left home she had muttered to him that she was only trying to stop him looking a fool. Perhaps he did look silly wearing them and Aunt Dorothy was just too kind-hearted to admit it.

"Cor! Look at that!" exclaimed a familiar voice, and Nicholas turned to find Louie behind him, wearing a frilly dress with roses on it, and with a pink bow perched on top of her wild curls.

The exhibition was in three partitioned sections, and Nicholas spent a long time in the first one where the theme was 'The Rat Attacks'. There were greatly-magnified photographs of rat-damage: a gas pipe gnawed through; a loaf of bread reduced to a hollow shell; a chair leg half eaten away. Rats had been caught by the camera in grain sacks, on kitchen tables, in trouser pockets—their images enlarged to terrifying proportions.

"Cor!" exclaimed Louie again. "What'd you do if you met one of them in the dark, little 'un?"

"He'd crawl under a bush, mos' likely," a thin voice piped up in the background, and Tommy's scrubbed, jeering face poked out from behind Louie.

"Shut you up," his sister said mildly. "Go an' stand with Mam. We're headin' for Aunty Connie's over in Larting," she explained to Nicholas. "Jes' popped in here for a quick look."

Nicholas could see now that the smart woman to whom Aunt Dorothy was talking just inside the doorway was in fact Mrs Bugg who had discarded her flowery apron and turban for a blue dress and a little round white hat.

"Where's Morna?" Louie asked, glancing anxiously towards her mother who looked as though she were about to leave.

"I think she's at the end, in 'Getting Rid Of The Rat'," Nicholas told her, moving on to 'We Attack The Rat' in the central section.

'MORE PEOPLE ARE KILLED BY RATS and the Work of Rats Than in All Wars Put Together,' a six-foot high poster told him. On the next panel there were smaller posters bearing sinister messages, such as, 'A Rat-Bite Can Kill within a Week!' and, 'A Rat's Trail Is a Tale of Disease'.

By now Nicholas could not feel sorry even when he saw photographs of rats in traps, or rats killed by ferrets, dogs, and cats. When he arrived at 'Getting Rid Of The Rat' and read that the only way to do this was by having the Council Rodent Operator bring his poison, he felt extremely grateful to that gentleman. He had been photographed three times, swinging merrily along with a bucket of white stuff, a long pole, and a sack.

Morna, looking flushed and excited after her talk with Louie, was waiting outside the door for Nicholas to join her. (Aunt Dorothy was rushing round the exhibition making disgusted faces at the photographs.)

"I'm going to Louie's tomorrow after shopping," Morna announced immediately. "I'm taking my lunch with me so I can eat it there. Mrs Bugg said I could. And after lunch we're going to teach those Footers a proper lesson! I'm to be the leader of the Buggs."

Already Nicholas had a sinking feeling in his stomach at the thought of being left on his own next day. He was determined not to show it, though.

"I'm going to have my lunch up at the farm with that nice land-girl, Shirley," he said, making up a story on the spur of the moment. "She said I could ride on the tractor with her tomorrow."

"You're telling a fib, Nicholas Newton! You are not!" Morna exclaimed furiously.

"I am!"

"You are not! You're a fibber! And you're a coward! So there!"

"I'm not! I'm not!"

"You are!"

"Children!" protested Aunt Dorothy's shocked voice behind them. She shooed them across the grass from the hall towards the road.

"I've never heard you two squabbling like this before," she said. "The Saxford air must be infecting you."

"It's his fault!" snapped Morna.

"It's not!" said Nicholas. "It's hers! She's a know-all. Bridget said so."

"He's a fibber, and a cow . . ."

Before she could finish Aunt Dorothy had gripped them both by their hands.

"Enough!" she said firmly, as they started home along the dusty road. "I'm sick of hearing about people quarrelling. You would have thought that after a six years' war we would all have been glad of a bit of peace!"

"Has someone else been quarrelling, then?" Morna asked inquisitively.

"Who never stops quarrelling?" sighed Aunt Dorothy. "The Footers and the Buggs of course! It's becoming really nasty now. Mrs Bugg has just been telling me about the latest development. Do you two know Charlie Bugg, Louie's cousin?"

Nicholas and Morna said that they did.

"Well," Aunt Dorothy went on, "Charlie's father, James,

39

keeps poultry. And because he has more than twenty-five hens, he's only supposed to sell his eggs to the packing-station. He doesn't, though. He sells them round the village at two pence apiece. And now Les Footer, Spikey's father, has reported him, so he has to appear in court shortly, and probably pay a large fine."

"And hasn't he any money?" asked Nicholas. "Will it ruin him?" He knew from reading that ruined people and their families were almost instantly reduced to begging, and he was trying to imagine what he would say if Charlie appeared in rags at the kitchen door.

"It's not so much that," Aunt Dorothy pointed out. "It's the effect it's going to have on the village as a whole. We'll have Footers punching Buggs in The Swan, the wives arguing in the butcher's, and the youngsters half-killing one another in the street. There's going to be a horrid atmosphere."

"Yes," Nicholas agreed fervently. "I'm glad we don't live right in the village."

That night Nicholas, wearing his leaden boots, was pursued along a black passageway by the gigantic Man in the Iron Mask. The Man had been after Nicholas for some three years now, ever since he had come across a book of that name (he had never actually looked inside it) on the second-bottom shelf in Gramarye's study. He woke up, shivering and drenched in sweat, to find Aunt Dorothy sitting on his bed with her torch in her hand, and Morna standing, silent and grim-faced beside her.

"Gosh!" said Aunt Dorothy, gently but cheerfully. "That was a horror, Sir Nicholas! Do you have these often?"

"Quite a lot," he admitted, too exhausted to feel embarrassed.

"I wonder why Bridget didn't warn me," Aunt Dorothy frowned.

"Bridget didn't know," Morna put in.

"Really!" said Aunt Dorothy. Then she raised the torch so that she could see Morna's face more clearly. "Well, it's nothing to be ashamed of," she added sharply. "Nightmares run in the Taylor family, you know. Your mother and I were both pestered by them until we were about twelve." She went off to make them all some hot milk, and Morna climbed back into bed.

"Do you think I might be more of a Taylor than a Newton, Morna?" Nicholas asked suddenly.

"It seems very likely," Morna replied, adding under her breath, "I'm certainly glad I'm not!"

9

Loner

Up to the last minute Nicholas continued to hope that Morna would relent and not leave him after all. She had gone out of her way to be generous to him this morning, slipping a quarter of her orange on to his plate at breakfast and allowing him to bounce her much-prized tennis ball all the way down to the shops and back again.

As soon as they returned from their shopping, however, she hurried into the kitchen to ask Mrs Bugg if she would please make up her packed lunch as she had shortly to be going. When he heard this, Nicholas felt a sharp pain in his throat, as though he had swallowed a piece of glass, then a sickly sort of emptiness inside.

"Won't you want a packed lunch, too, Nick?" Morna asked with a cruel, little gleam in her eye. "I thought you were having a picnic with that land-girl up at the farm."

"I decided not to," said Nicholas, biting his lip to stop its treacherous quivering.

Morna eyed him coolly for a moment. "You could come with me, you know," she stated finally. "If you didn't want to fight, you could run with messages or tend the wounded. The Quakers did that in the war. Gramarye told me."

Nicholas wavered and almost succumbed. Then the

stubborn streak which he seemed to have acquired in the past twenty-four hours reasserted itself. I don't want to go. So why should I? he thought.

"I'd rather stay here," he said. He even succeeded in smiling a little. "I'll play at being Robinson Crusoe before he meets Friday."

It was Morna's turn to feel hurt. "Please yourself then," she said in a tight voice as she walked off to the gate, shoulders drooping. Just before she disappeared, however, her head shot round and she hurled a final insult. "Please yourself, if you want to play the coward, Nicholas Newton!"

Now that Morna had gone, Nicholas felt hot pinpoints pricking behind his eyes and the lump in his throat swelling ominously. Was he really a coward just because he did not want to be punched and kicked by a bunch of stupid boys? He shuffled unhappily round to the orchard and flung himself face-down in the long, cool grass. He pulled his fingers again and again through the soft blades, making them squeak. He was trying to think of something he might do to prove to himself that he was not a coward. He lay there for some time before an idea came to him. When it did, he jumped to his feet, anxious to put himself to the test as soon as possible.

"Mrs Bugg! Could I have a packed lunch, too?" he started, as he pushed the back door open. Then he stopped in confusion, for Mrs Bugg was not darting around happily in a haze of cigarette smoke as usual, but was sitting at the table, dabbing her red eyes with a handkerchief. Aunt Dorothy stood beside her, one hand laid comfortingly on her shoulder.

"It's all right, Nicholas," Aunt Dorothy said reassuringly. "Mrs Bugg's upset about Simon. He's gone off with his tent again. It's what he does when things get too much for him. I'm telling her she mustn't worry. He always turns up safe and sound."

Mrs Bugg gave Nicholas a watery smile and sniffed loudly. "I knows he can't help it, poor lad," she said, "but he fares like to break his mother's heart. That he do! What with walkin' around like a stat-yer, never openin' his lips, an' takin' hisself off every few weeks, the good Lord knows where!"

"Perhaps he's been upset by all this new trouble between the Buggs and the Footers," Aunt Dorothy suggested.

"More than likely," Mrs Bugg agreed. "He listen, you know, settin' there in his corner, though he say nothin'. An' he never did take kindly to fightin' an' feudin' even when he were a little lad like Tommy. That used to make him real angry. Waste o' time, he'd say it were. He'd rather a bin bird-spottin' or fishin' or lookin' for butterflies. Reckon he musta hated th'army. But he went voluntary, you know, Mrs Buchanan."

"I know. He's a good lad," Aunt Dorothy said soothingly. As she spoke she was deftly placing bread, margarine, a lettuce, and grated cheese on the table. "We'll just have to be patient," she added, as she moved towards the door. "Time's a great healer, Mrs Bugg."

When she had gone, Mrs Bugg gave a final tremulous sigh, then set about making Nicholas's sandwiches. "Yes. He always were a deep one," she said thoughtfully as she spread the first slice of bread. "Always a loner were our Simon. That's hard on a loner sometimes. Specially in a place like Saxford."

I suppose I'm a loner too, now, thought Nicholas, as he hurried along the edge of the wheat field, carrying his lunch in an old army knapsack he had found in the junk room. It was a sultry day of low cloud with the landscape drained of colour, and even the larks' singing sounded melancholy. He tried to imagine Morna in the black army hut with all the Buggs around her, talking and laughing. He knew that Mrs Bugg had given her two biscuits with her sandwiches, and now he wondered jealously whether she would give one to Louie. It was really horrid of her to have left him like this, he thought, with a sudden spurt of anger. Then he began to feel abysmally sorry for himself, and that feeling lasted until he had crossed the ditch, crawled through the hedge, and was standing in the wood.

From then on his spirits lifted considerably because the test he had devised for himself was now very close and would soon be behind him. It was the same elation he always felt in the dentist's waiting room in the final minutes before he was called into the surgery. No matter how much he had moaned, or carried on, or flung himself about beforehand, when the ordeal was upon him he almost ran to meet it. Now he ran to the gate which stood between him and Colonel Cutworth's bunker. He squeezed through the lower part of it with no difficulty, brushing away the tendrils of barbed wire which dangled half-heartedly from the top bar. Then he walked, soft-footed, scarcely daring to breathe, his heart bounding violently once when a large bird flew out of the bushes with a great squawking and beating of wings.

The bunker was only a little distance along the track at the end of what looked like a short railway-cutting running into the side of the wooded slope. Nicholas's legs became a shade wobbly as he forced himself to walk up to the bunker's open, cave-like entrance. What if Colonel Cutworth kept a watch on the place? He imagined the colonel looking like the photographs of Grandfather Newton which Gramarye had in her study: handsome but stern, with a white moustache and bright, sharp eyes—a gentleman who would brook no nonsense and who would never understand about Nicholas's test.

No one challenged him, however, even when he took a step into the bunker's musty-smelling blackness which dropped over him so suddenly that he felt as though he were being suffocated as well as blinded. The thought of taking another step into it was terrifying. There might be anything—or anybody—in there! Even Morna would shrink from walking into this black void. He had to do it, though. Had to. This was the test. After he had done it he would feel wonderful, he told himself, just like he felt when he came out of the dentist's. He gritted his teeth, put his right hand against what felt like a brick wall, and started inching his way along.

After a bit he found that it helped if he pretended that his imaginary brother, Victor, were by his side.

"Well, Vic, we haven't knocked against anything, yet," he said out loud, (since there seemed no fear of anyone overhearing him).

"No," Victor's voice replied inside Nicholas's head. "There seems to be nothing but the four walls. We've just reached a corner, haven't we?"

"Yes. But hold on! There's a door here in this back wall. It isn't locked, either. The handle's turning."

"Gosh! I wouldn't go in, though, Nick! We might get well and truly lost, if we did that. One room's enough for the test. One room and eating your lunch just outside the doorway."

"All right, Vic. If you say so. Another corner coming up! We'll soon be back where we started."

When he did finally find his hand waving in empty space, and realized that he had come back to the entrance, he felt weak with relief. He lurched out into the daylight, hastily pulled the knapsack off over his head, and began to eat as quickly as he could. One sandwich, a biscuit and an apple would be enough to ensure that he passed the test, he decided. He was not feeling particularly hungry anyway. Having forced the food down, he set off at a run towards the gate, dived through it, and flung himself on his back on the path. He had done it. Three cheers for Nicholas Newton! He had proved that he was not a coward! That stupid sister of his could just take back what she had said about him. A lop-sided somersault landed him back on his feet, and he went bounding along the path, the knapsack flapping up and down as though it were patting him approvingly on the back.

When Nicholas arrived back at the cottage ten minutes later, though, his elation soon faded. Mrs Bugg had gone home, and had it not been for the tiny, faraway chattering of Aunt Dorothy's typewriter, he might have thought the place was completely deserted. He found a note from his aunt on the kitchen table telling him that there was milk and biscuits in the larder. "Frightfully busy!" it finished. "See you at five. Love, Aunt D." Nicholas sighed, dropped his knapsack on a chair and went out.

The nagging ache, caused by Morna abandoning him, numbed while he had been in the woods, now started up again. He wandered round aimlessly, feeling more and more depressed. Then, in the corner of the orchard, he spotted Simon Bugg's thick gardening-gloves and the scythe with which he had been mowing the grass. He picked them up dutifully and carried them across the yard to the old stable where he knew the gardening tools were stored. He pulled the sticking door open with some effort and threw the scythe and gloves inside. Immediately there was a scuffle, then a loud crash from the back where the cans of paraffin were stored.

Nicholas shut the door hastily, his heart drumming. Someone was hiding in there! Was it Simon Bugg? Had he not gone off with his tent, after all? And if it wasn't Simon, who else could it be? Some tramp? Did tramps still roam the countryside? He knew that they used to, because he had often read about them in stories. He backed across the yard to lean against the cottage wall beneath the bathroom window. If the worst came to the worst, he could hammer on the glass, he thought, and Aunt Dorothy might hear him.

As Nicholas stared at the handle of the stable door, watching fearfully for it to turn, his eye was suddenly caught by a movement lower down. From under the door a grey shape was emerging. At first he thought it was a mouse. Then as the intruder's bright, sharp eyes sized him up, and decided he could be safely ignored, he realized his mistake. Too large for a mouse, and too bold, it sat on the cobbles calmly grooming itself.

"A rat!" Nicholas whispered.

Oddly enough he felt no revulsion, for this rat looked nothing like the beady-eyed, bloated horrors he had seen at the exhibition. It was small and thin, its grey back distinctively marked by a 'V' of lighter hairs which came to a point between its ears. It performed its toilet unhurriedly, looking up at him occasionally.

Nicholas could not decide whether a rat would be sufficient reason for him to disturb Aunt Dorothy. Supposing he did and it had gone by the time she came to see it? She might be very annoyed. She might even think he had imagined it. He remembered how Bridget had once insisted that he had imagined a brown, growling dog in Gramarye's garden when, in fact, it had jumped over the fence into Mrs Rawlinson-Fox's whilst Nicholas was looking for help. In the end he thought he would wait until five o'clock to tell Aunt Dorothy about the rat.

Suddenly he jumped, for the rat had darted forward. To his relief, however, he saw that it was heading not for him but for a fragment of coal that it had spied on the cobbles. It lifted it between its two front paws and began gnawing at it voraciously.

Poor thing! It must be starving, Nicholas thought compassionately. At the same time he remembered that he had an apple core in his trouser pocket. He looked around him. There was no one to see him. Anyway, he told himself, he might easily have dropped the apple core accidentally, in which case the rat would have found it. He drew it slowly from his pocket and bowled it along the ground.

To begin with he thought that he had merely chased the rat away for, frightened by the sudden movement, it darted off towards the outhouses. Before it reached them, though, it stopped and turned round, its nose twitching. Then, very slowly and cautiously, it began to creep back, almost on its belly, towards the apple core. In a flash it had it in its mouth and was running off to wherever its home might be, out of the yard and down by the side of the stable.

Nicholas looked after it with mixed feelings of benevolence and guilt. He knew deep down that he should not have given it food. But perhaps now that it had found something to eat it would not need to come back again, he told himself. It was a very little rat and looked quite young. It had probably strayed into the yard by accident. I won't tell Aunt Dorothy about it just yet, he decided, as he walked round to the kitchen door. If I see it here again, I'll tell her. But I wonder whether I ought to tell Morna . . .

Unable to make up his mind on this point, he drank his milk, finished off what was left of his lunch, then (perhaps because rats were on his mind) chose *The Wind in the Willows* to take into the orchard with him, to pass the time until he should have someone to talk to.

10

A Pleasant Evening

Morna was flushed with self-importance although, as it turned out, there had been no Footers around that afternoon to fight.

"The trouble with the Buggs is that they have no idea about military strategy," she declared, as she returned from dropping her dirty socks in the laundry basket in the bathroom. "That's why, with my background, I'm so very useful to them, you know."

"Do you mean because you've had so much practice at pretend-fighting in our games?" Nicholas asked. He was sitting cross-legged on his pillow with Nooka, the monkey, tucked under his arm, wishing that Morna would finish talking so that he could tell her about the bunker and the rat before teatime. She had burst in on him as he sat in the orchard, ten minutes before, and had not stopped talking since.

"No! Of course not," she replied, looking pained. "I wish you'd stop talking about pretend-fighting, Nick! It sounds so babyish . . . What I meant was that I've got soldiering in my blood, being a Newton. Things like spotting a good place for an ambush come naturally to me. The Buggs and the Footers think fighting just means rushing at one another and punching and kicking."

"I've noticed," said Nicholas with feeling.

"It's much more fun than that," observed Morna, pushing her dusty feet into her sandals. "I'm setting up a proper headquarters for them in Louie's room, and we're going to have maps, and plan our forays . . . You ought to have come down to the Buggs' place, Nick," she went on without pausing for breath. "It's lovely what they've done with that old hut!

48

Cousin Charlie's dad has made all these wooden partitions, like walls, so they can each have their own private room; and they have lots of pictures pinned up, and vases of flowers everywhere, and red and blue curtains, the same material as Mrs Bugg's pinafore. That's really pretty!"

"You sounded just like Louie Bugg!" Nicholas pointed out sharply. "You said 'that' instead of 'it'."

"Did I? It must be catching." Morna gave her high, rippling laugh and looked quite pleased.

"What's catching?" Aunt Dorothy asked, in pretended alarm, as she looked in from the lobby. "Not measles, mumps, or chickenpox, I hope!"

"No," explained Nicholas. "Louie Bugg's 'thats'. . . *That's* real pretty!" he mimicked in a high voice, holding Nooka up to protect his head as Morna hurled her pillow at him.

"Oh, dear!" laughed Aunt Dorothy as she led the way into the kitchen for tea. "Gramarye and Bridget will be after my blood if you catch Suffolk accents. You must promise not to write in them."

"Nick won't catch one, anyway," Morna declared, her eyes lighting up at the sight of her favourite meat-and-potato pie. "He doesn't want to play with my friends in the village."

"I didn't say I didn't want to *play* with them," Nicholas observed, staring hard at Morna until she turned red. They both knew that if Aunt Dorothy discovered that Morna was involving herself in the Footer-Bugg feud there would be trouble.

"Actually I think it would be a good idea if you did try to make friends in the village, too, Sir Nicholas," Aunt Dorothy said kindly as she passed Nicholas the bread. "It can't be very pleasant for you wandering around on your own. Besides, you'll be going to school when your mother and father come home. So it will break you in, if you mix with other children and learn how to stick up for yourself."

"Going to school!" Morna and Nicholas echoed in unison, Morna in a delighted, Nicholas in a profoundly shocked tone.

"Yes." Aunt Dorothy smiled. "Of course you will! You

49

didn't think you were going to escape it for ever, did you?"

"I've always wanted to go to school," Morna declared. "It was so boring, just Nick and me with that horrid Miss Stearne. There was a school not far from Gramarye's, and we used to watch them playing in the yard."

"Gramarye said we would get fleas, or the itch, or beasts in our hair if we went to school," Nicholas put in.

"I'll be all right. But I expect you will get fleas," Morna told him cheerfully. "He gets fleas so easily," she explained to Aunt Dorothy. "He even caught them when we went to see *Snow-White,* and we were in the most expensive seats, too."

"Oh, I'm sure there will be a flea-less school somewhere that will be able to accommodate Sir Nicholas," Aunt Dorothy told them. "He might even come to like it in a few hundred years."

Nicholas was wondering whether fleas, like nightmares, ran in the Taylor family.

"Do you ever have fleas, Aunt Dorothy?" he asked as he passed her the sugar bowl.

"I've always preferred this," she replied, straight-faced. "With just a spot of milk, or sometimes lemon."

Morna laughed so hard that she choked and had to be thumped on the back by Aunt Dorothy. Nicholas laughed at Morna's choking. And Aunt Dorothy laughed at them both. By the time the laughing was over they all had unattractive, scarlet faces and bleary eyes (Morna even had a nose-drip) but they felt very pleasant inside. Nicholas was in such good spirits that he did not even start worrying about going to school. Nor did he feel irritated when Louie Bugg appeared at the door as they were washing the dishes.

Louie, who seemed to live in a state of breathless excitement, looked wilder and dustier than ever this evening. "Tommy an' Charlie an' me's goin' into Bury tomorrow mornin' to git a message fer Uncle James," she gasped. "Thought Morna might fancy comin', too. That'll be quiet, bein' a Thursday, Mrs Buchanan."

"Oh, yes!" exclaimed Morna, clapping two forks together

in the towel with which she was drying them, and bouncing up and down. "May I go? Please, Aunt Dorothy!"

"I don't see why not. I've been meaning to take you both in to see the town myself, and haven't got round to it," Aunt Dorothy replied, absentmindedly ruffling Louie's curls while she contemplated Nicholas. "Isn't Nicholas invited, too, though?"

"Course he is, if he want to come," Louie said amiably.

"Do you want to go, Nicholas?" asked Aunt Dorothy.

"Oh, do come, Nick!" Morna urged him, still bouncing.

"Yes, thank you," agreed Nicholas, feeling more cheered than ever, now that he saw that Morna did still want his company.

"Meet you outside the church, then. That's where the bus stops. Half arter nine," Louie said as she headed for the door. Having just caught her breath she was already getting up steam for the return journey. "See yer, Mrs Buchanan! See yer, Morna! See yer, little 'un!" she called hoarsely as she vanished.

Nicholas and Morna helped their aunt cut lettuces after that, to take down to Mrs Nelson at the stores who sold them for her, so that it was bedtime before Nicholas had a chance to tell Morna what he had done that afternoon. They had climbed into their beds, and he was just starting on his story when Aunt Dorothy came hurrying in with a torch for Nicholas to keep under his pillow in case of nightmares. By the time she had gone Morna was already lying down, her hair, loosed from its plaits, spread over her pillow in a dark, rippling fan.

"Morna! Did you hear me?" Nicholas whispered. "You'll never guess where I went today! I went through that gate in the wood—the one with all the 'Danger' notices on it—and right inside the colonel's bunker. I really did! So I can't be a coward. Can I?"

"M-m-m."

"And do you know what I saw later, round in the yard, coming out of the old stable. An enormous rat! Well, it wasn't actually enormous, it was quite little. But it was a rat! Should I have told Aunt Dorothy?"

51

"M-m-m."

"Morna?"

Silence.

She did hear me, though, thought Nicholas, smiling cynic-
ally. She just doesn't want to apologise. That's Morna Newton
all over!

11

In Disgrace

By the following morning Nicholas was feeling much less
enthusiastic about his trip into Bury with the Buggs.

I expect Morna will stick with Louie all the time, he reflected
gloomily as he ate his cornflakes, and Tommy will be with
Charlie. I'll be the odd one out. Nevertheless he felt he could
not back out now, so he tried to look reasonably cheerful as
Aunt Dorothy inspected them before they left to make sure
they were clean and tidy.

She gave them a shilling each to spend, as well as their bus
fares.

"Do be careful of the traffic," she told them. "There are still
a lot of jeeps roaring about the town. And you *will* keep an eye
on Nicholas, Morna, won't you?"

"I always do," Morna sighed long-sufferingly.

Although they left the cottage in plenty of time, Morna
insisted that they run all the way to the village in case the bus
arrived early. Consequently they were both breathless and
uncomfortably sticky by the time they reached the deserted
bus stop outside the church.

"Never mind! It's the early bird that catches the worm,"
gasped Morna, hoisting herself up on to the churchyard wall.

"I thought it was a bus we were catching," Nicholas panted,

with a brave attempt at jollity. Now that they were so close to joining the Buggs, he felt less than ever inclined to be with them.

Three of the village women, wearing hats and gloves because they were going to town, came sauntering along to the stop. They were followed by the tall, thin young man who sometimes helped out in the post office. Then finally, just when Morna was growing anxious, and Nicholas hopeful, the Buggs appeared, marching up from the green in Indian file with Louie in the lead.

Louie was wearing her dress with the roses on it, whilst the two boys had on shirts of such a dazzling whiteness that it made their faces look browner and more ferret-like than ever, Nicholas thought.

"Here you are together, then!" Louie observed with a wide grin as she came striding up to them. "Bin here long?"

"Yes, for ages!" replied Morna, anxious to impress on Louie their eagerness to be part of the Bugg expedition. "We didn't want to be late, you see."

"Didn't think little old Four-eyes'd be a-comin'. Did you, Charlie?" Tommy muttered to his cousin, but loudly enough to ensure that Nicholas heard him. "Reckon we'd better see if there ain't a bush handy fer when that darned grit bus come roarin' along."

"Think he'll be scared?" Charlie tittered.

"Scared! He's scared of his own shadow! Proper little yellow cowardy-custard he is!" sneered Tommy, looking Nicholas up and down contemptuously.

A seething began inside of Nicholas, gentle at first—a mere bubbling round the edges—but gradually boiling up more and more furiously until, without quite knowing how it had come about, he found himself holding Tommy Bugg by the shoulders and shaking him violently to and fro.

"You shut up! And don't dare call me a coward!" he was yelling. "Just don't ever say that again!"

Then, somewhere behind his own voice, he heard a ripping sound. The sleeve of Tommy's snow-white shirt came away

53

in his hand. And he staggered back, off balance, against the wall.

There was a minute's total silence before Tommy let out a high wail, and Louie an astounded "Corblast!"

"His best shirt!" exclaimed Charlie in a funereal tone. "Auntie Mabel'll throw a fit!"

The three women now crowded round, attracted by the dramatic sounds issuing from Tommy's wide-open mouth.

"My godfathers! Who done that?" demanded the stoutest, gaping at the boy's exposed arm.

"Him! It were him!" Charlie cried, pointing an accusing finger at Nicholas.

"One of them toffs from the farm-cottage," the woman next to the stout one muttered waspishly.

"That's surely Mabel Bugg's little 'un!" the third woman suddenly exclaimed, bending down to peer at Tommy's face. "That is! Ain't that jes' like it?" she demanded of her companions. "As if poor Mabel didn't have a barrerload o' troubles already without that some vicious bully-boy come a-tearin' the shirt off her little 'un's back!"

"An' we've hardly no clothin' coupons left neither!" exclaimed Louie in an excited, trembly voice.

The women made a variety of sympathetic noises as the bus came into view.

"We can't go inter town now," said Louie glumly. "Not with Tommy lookin' like that."

"Git you along home, my old love! Tell your mam what's happened," advised the stout woman, darting Nicholas a poisonous look as she hauled herself on to the bus behind her friends.

Nicholas had been standing in what must have looked like a stupor for several minutes now. In fact, though, he had seen and heard all too clearly what had been going on around him. It was only the power of speech and movement that had deserted him from the moment of the sleeve's coming away in his hand. Inside his head he had been yelling at all these angry faces that it had been an accident; that he had not meant to tear

54

Tommy's shirt; that it had all been Tommy Bugg's fault in the first place for making him lose his temper. Since his lips would not open, however, or his voice box function, he had had to stand there dumbly and let the recriminations and the hard looks rain down on him.

Suddenly Morna spoke for the first time. "You'd best come up to Aunt Dorothy's. Your mother will be there," she said.

Although her remark was obviously directed at Louie and Tommy, her screwed-up eyes were not looking at them but into the churchyard, and Nicholas saw, to his dismay, that her face was very red and her lower lip trembling. The enormity of what he had done really came home to him then: Morna on the point of tears! Nicholas had known Morna to shed tears in public only once; and that had been when Bridget had taken them to see a film called *Dumbo,* which had been so sad that almost every child in the cinema had been crying.

"Come along, Nicholas," she said in a flat, hopeless voice, leading the way across the road, her chin sunk on her chest and her shoulders drooping.

Tommy snatched his sleeve back from Nicholas, and the three Buggs set off after Morna, with Nicholas trailing a little way behind them. The procession dragged its sombre way back to the cottage with Nicholas feeling more like a criminal at every step. If the others did talk, it was in low, solemn voices, as though they might be discussing his execution. It was almost a relief when they arrived at the white gate. Morna stood aside with bowed head to usher the others in ahead of her.

"We had better wait outside until they break the news," she said dolefully and gazed at a point above Nicholas's head, as though she could not bear to look at his face.

"That's not fair," he objected, stung at last into speaking up for himself. "I won't have a chance of telling my side."

"You haven't got a side," Morna stated grimly. "You've done a terrible thing and will have to take what's coming to you."

What came, a few minutes later, was Aunt Dorothy in a

furious temper, brandishing the pen she had been using when Mrs Bugg had arrived at the study door with her tale of woe. She informed Nicholas very loudly (in a voice that was not quite a shout) that he was a naughty, vicious-tempered, little boy, who ought to be ashamed of himself, and that he was to go to his room and stay there until she told him he could come out.

"But that's not fair!" Nicholas protested again.

He walked uncertainly towards his aunt, his head whirling at the shocking injustice of what had happened to him. Aunt Dorothy had told him only last night that he must learn to stick up for himself. And when he did just that, this was how she treated him!

"You must learn to control your temper, Nicholas," Aunt Dorothy said severely. "I'm afraid you've been very spoiled . . . Now run along to your room when you're told!"

Nicholas turned in desperation to Morna, but she was still avoiding his eyes. Her shoulders were hunched and her head poked forward a little as she gazed down the orchard.

"You look just like a vulture standing there. Did you know that?" Nicholas said with a brittle little laugh before he swaggered off to the front door (thus avoiding the Buggs) and along to their bedroom. There he banged the door shut behind him and immediately burst into tears.

12

V for Victor

It was Morna's betrayal that hurt Nicholas most of all. Although he did not feel very kindly towards Aunt Dorothy, he could make allowances for her. She did not know what a nasty piece of work Tommy Bugg was. She had not seen what actually did happen at the bus stop as Morna had. Certainly it did not say much for her that she was prepared to take the word of strangers against that of her own nephew. But this was treachery of a very pale colour compared with Morna's! Never once in all Morna's tussles with Bridget had he failed to stand by her. Many times he had even shared in her punishment of his own free will. And now she could let him down like this!

Nicholas considered several forms of revenge during the long hours of his solitary confinement that morning. Poking Anastasia's eyes in. Tearing out the last pages of Morna's favourite books. Cutting off the heads of the paper-dolls that Louie had given her. In the end, however, he satisfied himself with throwing her tennis ball out of the window and muddling up her books so that the best ones were in the dark corner at the back of the cupboard, and the worst ones at the front. Then he sat on his bed with Nooka and *The Wind in the Willows* and waited sullenly for his release.

He waited and waited, but no one came to free him. He finished 'The Open Road' chapter and started on 'The Wild Wood'. His stomach rumbled more and more persistently. Suddenly an appalling idea came to him. Was Aunt Dorothy going to keep him without food? Would she do such a heartless thing to appease Mrs Bugg? There was no clock in the room so he had no idea what the time was. He tiptoed across to the door, opened it, and listened. There was not a sound to be heard anywhere.

Tight-lipped, Nicholas marched along the lobby, through the living room, and into the empty kitchen. The clock on the wall told him that it was quarter past two. The round wooden tray which Aunt Dorothy used for her meals when she was working sat on the otherwise bare kitchen table. It held a plate of cold mutton, cold new potatoes, and carrot. Was it his aunt's lunch, Nicholas wondered. Then he decided that he did not care whose it was. He was weak with hunger and he was going to eat it! It was not right to starve anyone for accidentally tearing a shirt. As he rapidly cleared the plate, he thought of Morna again, and of how she must have sat enjoying her lunch, knowing that her brother was alone, miserable and hungry. She's worse than Marie-Antoinette, he reflected bitterly. (Morna and he had long ago agreed that stony-hearted Marie-Antoinette was their least favourite historical character.)

When he had finished eating, he dumped his dirty plate defiantly in the sink, and went out. There was no one to be seen or heard, although he supposed that Aunt Dorothy must be working in her study. He decided to walk across to the far corner of the yard where he could listen for the sound of her typewriter. Even though she was a cruel and unjust aunt, it would be reassuring to know that she was within call, and that he had not been totally abandoned.

Just as he reached the bathroom window his heart skipped a beat as something darted across his path. That rat, again! There it was, hardly bigger than a mouse, sitting in front of the stable door, watching him with its small, diamond eyes. He knew it was the same rat because of the V-mark on its back. What a nerve it had.

"Go away!" he shouted angrily.

The rat's whiskers twitched, but it remained where it was.

Nicholas looked round for something to throw and saw a small, red fragment of drainpipe. He picked it up and hurled it, but it fell short, and the rat darted forward to pick it up in its teeth. Then it dropped it and looked up at Nicholas reproachfully.

"Oh, no!" he exclaimed with sudden comprehension. "You thought I was feeding you again! Is that why you've come?" He was stricken with remorse. The rat had come to search him out, and he had repaid its trust by trying to hurt it.

He clapped his hands and stamped his foot, hoping to frighten it away. Still it stood its ground. Then, all at once, it gave a small, plaintive squeal. Nicholas could hardly believe it. It was actually asking him to feed it! He made a little rush forward, shouting, "Shoo!" in desperation. All that happened was that the rat moved a few feet away to the right, then gave another little squeal.

Nicholas felt common sense being edged out by pity. What

58

would be the harm in feeding one small rat? he asked himself. In fact why shouldn't he tame it? He had heard about people in prison taming wild mice or rats for company. It would give him something to do, instead of wandering around on his own every day. He wouldn't let it come too close, of course, in case it bit him accidentally. But he could still have fun with it from a distance.

"Hold on, Ratty!" he told it, suddenly making up his mind.

Rushing off to the kitchen he was back a moment later with a two-day-old scone that he had found in the breadbin. He began feeding it to the rat which had not moved from the spot where he had left it. Whenever he threw a piece down, it seized it and carried it off to eat it just round the corner of the stable. When the scone was finished, Nicholas held out his empty hands. "All gone!" he called, as though he were talking to a small child. "Look, Ratty! All gone!"

The rat stared at him for a moment, then, as though it understood, it sat down and began to wash its face.

"You're very intelligent," Nicholas said admiringly. "You deserve a proper name, really." He thought for a moment, then murmured, "Vee? Because of that mark on your back? Vee . . . for victory?"

The rat was grooming behind its ears now.

"I know what I'll call you!" Nicholas cried with a sudden flash of inspiration. "Victor! Like my pretend-brother. 'V' for Victor!"

At that moment there was a sudden burst of noisy, excited talking somewhere at the back of the cottage, followed by Aunt Dorothy's anxious voice calling, "Nicholas! Nicholas! Where are you?"

Victor whisked his tail twice and was gone.

Nicholas walked reluctantly back across the yard and round to the kitchen door. He found Aunt Dorothy and Morna standing there together.

"Nicholas!" exclaimed Aunt Dorothy, pressing her hand to her heart in relief. "We couldn't think where you were! Whenever did you have your lunch, love?"

"About quarter past two," Nicholas replied stiffly.

"Oh, dear!" groaned his aunt, putting her hands on his shoulders and steering him gently indoors. "I am sorry, Sir Nicholas! You must have thought I'd turned into a dragon-aunt! There's been a frightful mix-up," she went on apologetically. "I didn't stop for lunch, but I told Morna to call you at twelve-thirty."

"She didn't," said Nicholas grimly.

"I know," his aunt sighed. "Apparently Mrs Bugg got it into her head that I was taking your dinner to you on the tray. So, in the end, nobody did anything."

"I see," said Nicholas with a wounded smile.

"The shirt might be all right," Morna piped up, frowning at Nicholas to show him that he was not quite restored to her good books yet. "We've just taken it down to Mrs Nelson's sister who has a sewing machine, and she says she'll do her best with it . . . Aunt Dorothy will have to pay for it, of course."

"Never mind about that!" said Aunt Dorothy hurriedly. "We're going to forget all about that horrid old shirt. Let's go in and have beevers. Do you feel hungry yet, Sir Nick?"

"No. Not really," he replied shortly. Aunt Dorothy need not think she was going to win him round so easily, not after the way she had treated him that morning.

"Sure?" she asked anxiously. "There's a scone left. You could share it with Morna."

Nicholas experienced a sinking feeling. He should have known that Aunt Dorothy would not have forgotten about the scone! Why had he not cut Victor a slice from the loaf instead?

"I've had the scone," he admitted, hastily averting his eyes from the Bread Code on the wall.

"Have you?" Aunt Dorothy smiled. "Well, I can't blame you—poor starving old thing! Morna can find something else."

Nicholas could feel Morna's eyes on him as Aunt Dorothy made the tea. She had been silent for at least five minutes which

60

was unusual. When she finally spoke it was in her most conciliatory tone.

"We could play at Robinson Crusoe after beevers, Nick, if you liked," she suggested. "I expect you could manage Robinson by now. You've seen me do him often enough."

"No, thank you," Nicholas replied sharply. "I'm playing one of my own games—with Victor. We don't want any silly girls."

"Victor! Who's Victor?"

"He's my pretend-brother," said Nicholas. "He's a person you can rely on, that doesn't ever let you down. Wish he was real!" he finished feelingly, and watched Morna's uncertain smile turn into a scowl as the barb went home.

13

Best Friends

That evening, before they went to sleep, Morna told Nicholas that Louie Bugg was her best friend.

Nicholas sat straight up in bed. "Better than me?" he asked in a shaky voice.

"Don't be silly!" said Morna impatiently. "You're my brother!"

Nicholas did not understand what she meant. As he saw it, until they had come to Aunt Dorothy's, Morna had undoubtedly been his best friend, and he had been hers.

"You're an arch-traitor, Morna Newton! That's what!" he pronounced in a voice charged with emotion.

"I wish you'd stop saying peculiar things like that," Morna grumbled. "You mustn't do it when we're with the others, anyway. It sounds so odd!"

"What others?"

"The Buggs, of course."

"I'm not having any more to do with them, thank you. And

you needn't bring them up here to play, either!" Nicholas said hotly, feeling for the comforting shape of the torch beneath his pillow.

"Please yourself," said Morna with a bleak smile. "I don't suppose they want the clothes torn from their backs, anyway."

Nicholas's head fell heavily on to his pillow. There was a single, low thud in his ear as though a heavy wooden curtain had dropped between him and Morna. He had been going to tell her about Victor the rat, too. Now he never would. She was leaving him and their shared secrets and games for Louie and the Buggs. Well, if that was what she wanted, let her go! He would just make a new life for himself, like Robinson Crusoe did when he was washed up on the island. After all he had the two Victors, and Nooka and his books.

That night, for the first time, he coped with a nightmare on his own. The fact that it was a new nightmare (giant bulls charging at him across a field where he stood helpless, literally rooted to the ground) seemed to emphasize the fact that he and his world were both changing inexorably. He lay on one elbow sweating, his torch switched on to banish the dark, pawing dream-shadows which still hovered round the edges of his consciousness, and he listened to Morna's quiet breathing. At first he was tempted to waken her, as he normally did, to be soothed by her grumpy, matter-of-fact reassurances. Then he felt again the new, hard core inside him growing a little, adding another layer of toughness. Morna did not want him. So he was not going to let her think that he needed her! He would manage on his own from now on.

It was some time before he could pluck up the courage to switch the torch off and close his eyes. When he did, however, he fell almost instantly into a dreamless sleep from which he had to be roused next morning by Morna's vigorous shaking. His first impulse was to tell her boastfully about his nightmare. Then he held back. Why should he tell her anything private now? She would only pass it on to her best friend, Louie Bugg!

"Well? And what are you two doing today?" Aunt Dorothy asked briskly at breakfast.

"Shopping and things in the morning," Morna replied. "Then going down to Louie's in the afternoon."

"I'm not," said Nicholas sharply. "Going down to Louie's, I mean."

"Nobody asked you," retorted Morna.

Aunt Dorothy bit her lip and looked vexed. "Now look here, you two," she started. "I don't like Nicholas being left on his own like this every afternoon. It makes me feel very guilty about him. Yet I just don't have time to keep him company. I must confess I didn't foresee this sort of problem when I agreed to have you both. Why can't you play together like you used to do?"

"I want to play with other people even if Nick doesn't. And Louie Bugg and I are best friends now," Morna said crossly.

"It's all right. Truly, Aunt Dorothy!" Nicholas said stoutly. "I like being on my own. I think I must be a loner, like Mrs Bugg says Simon is."

Aunt Dorothy stared at them both as though she were trying very hard to figure them out. Then she said reluctantly, "Well, I suppose if Nicholas insists that he's happy, I must take his word for it. Still, it's a pity he couldn't have found himself a best friend, too."

"Oh, but he has!" said Morna with a mocking gleam in her eye. "He has Victor."

"Victor?" Aunt Dorothy repeated, looking puzzled.

Nicholas's cornflake-loaded spoon stopped halfway to his mouth as he sat transfixed by shock and dismay. How had Morna found out about the rat? Had he been talking in his sleep?

"He has a pretend-brother, called Victor," Morna went on contemptuously. "He prefers him to real people."

Nicholas, feeling quite light-headed with relief, giggled nervously and spluttered cornflakes over the tablecloth.

"That's only because he hasn't had a chance to meet boys of his own sort," Aunt Dorothy said kindly as she cleared the table. "Once Sir Nicholas goes to school he'll make lots of friends."

Later, as they were returning from shopping, each carrying a bag up the long hill, Morna suddenly said, "As soon as we get back, you must go in and apologize to Mrs Bugg about Tommy's shirt, Nick."

"Oh, no! Aunt Dorothy said we could forget about that!" Nicholas wailed. He had been planning to skip elevenses for the very purpose of avoiding Mrs Bugg.

"You must!" Morna insisted, looking flushed and tight-lipped. "I told Mummy and Daddy in our letter last night about your tearing the shirt. I want to finish it tonight with telling how you apologized."

"You are a rotten sneak, Morna Newton! You really are!" Nicholas cried, seeing that he was trapped.

In the end, though, it turned out that Morna had done him a service. For when he did finally venture into the kitchen to stammer his apologies, he found to his relief that he had not, after all, lost Mrs Bugg's regard.

"That's all right, my little darlin'!" she said. "I were a bit het up when I seen that old shirt yesterday, an' I don't pretend I weren't. But I soon simmer down. 'That's jes' boys' nature,' I say to Louie . . . An' then, I reckon our Tommy musta goaded you some. He can be whoolly a torment when he like. Anyways, that's mended near as good as new now."

Nicholas, feeling a great surge of warmth towards Mrs Bugg, stayed to help her set out the elevenses. He noticed her lip tremble as she reached out automatically for Simon's cup, then had to withdraw her hand hastily.

"I expect he'll come home soon, Mrs Bugg," he said comfortingly.

"I surely hope so," Mrs Bugg replied as she poured out the tea. "That git me down some, Nicholas, I can tell you! Waitin' an' waitin' an' never a word. Yet Dr McLean say that's probably doin' our Simon the world o' good; the feelin' o' freedom an' the quiet an' all . . . 'Spect he's a-watchin' birds an' drawin' flowers. (He draws flowers a treat, you know.) Jes' hope he's findin' enough to eat without stealin'. That's what worry me! That'd kill him were he to be shoved in a prison again!"

"They wouldn't really put poor Simon Bugg in prison if he stole food to eat, would they, Aunt Dorothy?" Nicholas asked at lunchtime, after Mrs Bugg had gone home.

"One would hope not." His aunt frowned. "Not after what Simon's been through for his country! But you do meet with some very unfeeling magistrates. And stealing food is a very serious offence nowadays when we're facing a possible famine."

"Footers'd just love that!" remarked Morna with such venom that Nicholas saw Aunt Dorothy throw her a sharp glance.

Later, as Nicholas stood in the yard in the sunshine feeding Victor with pieces of biscuit, he remembered his aunt's words with a pang of unease. Right now, he himself was probably committing a serious offence. For not only had he taken food from his aunt's larder (he could not bring himself to use the word 'stolen') but he was feeding it to an enemy. ('Your New Enemy Is The Rat!' Wasn't that what the posters shouted at him?) Yet, watching Victor running busily back and forth with his pieces of biscuit, or sitting up to stare at him with his bright beady eyes, Nicholas did not feel that he was doing anything wrong. Victor was only a small, wild animal. He could not help it that he was one of the hated rat-tribe. If he managed to tame him properly, would he be allowed to keep him, Nicholas wondered. Could they have him disinfected to kill all the wild-rat germs? (Mrs Rawlinson-Fox's cat had been disinfected when it returned home after a three weeks' absence.)

I could make him a lovely house, Nicholas thought dreamily, throwing down the last fragment of biscuit. He would probably like some sort of tunnel to play in. The one from my train set might do. And a big pile of straw and sawdust to burrow into when he wants to be private. And bits of wood to gnaw. Perhaps a mirror, like birds have, for when he's washing his face . . . I could bring the tunnel out now to see how he likes it!

"You wait there, Victor . . ." he started. Then his voice

tailed off as he stood looking foolishly round the empty yard. Having realized that the food had come to an end, Victor had obviously taken himself off whilst Nicholas stood making his plans. The tunnel would have to be kept until tomorrow.

"But I can think about his house," Nicholas told himself. "And, with Morna out of the way, I can have a good look in the junk room to see if there's anything Victor might like to play with."

He was still in there, searching, when he became aware of Morna thumping around in their room, and realized to his astonishment that it must be almost teatime.

14

Spilled Blood

There were two boxes containing assorted small pieces of wood in the junk room, obviously saved by some handyman who had never found a use for them. With these, and odd bits from his train set, Nicholas laid out roadways, hurdles, and bridges on the cobbles, tempting Victor along different routes by strategically-placed fragments of food. His most valuable find, though, had been a peculiar yellow vase shaped like a very fat rolling-pin, with a pottery plug at one end and tiny holes along the top for the flower stems. When the plug was removed, this became an artificial burrow, into which Victor would dive enthusiastically and scrabble about so energetically that he rolled the vase over and over, as though he were performing a stunt.

Nicholas soon lost any early apprehensions he had about being discovered playing with Victor. But he did not take any risks. On Sunday afternoon, for example, when both Morna and Aunt Dorothy had been about, he had contented himself with rushing round to the yard to throw down some pieces of cake for Victor to find later. He soon discovered, too, that Victor could be relied upon to scamper off at the first hint of danger. This had been evident on Tuesday when Mrs Bugg and Aunt Dorothy had come round to the yard unexpectedly to fetch coal from the stable. Then Victor had dived for cover long before Nicholas had even heard the two women's foot-steps. Fortunately neither of them had shown any interest in what he was doing on the cobbles, obviously taking it for granted that he was playing one of his solitary games. In the end Nicholas decided that Morna, with her sharp eyes and her inquisitive nature, was really the only one he had to fear. And luckily she was too engrossed with the Buggs and their battles to care what Nicholas did with his afternoons.

Yet, ironically, because he was keeping Victor's existence a secret from Morna, Nicholas could not be entirely happy. Taming the rat was absorbing and exciting, and he ached often to share this excitement with his sister. He held back, not because he feared that Morna would give his secret away, but because she had already betrayed him by preferring Louie to himself. She had lost her right to share in his secrets, and he was determined that she should not have them back.

Morna, on the other hand, could hardly wait to be on her own with Nicholas every evening so that she could tell him in detail how she had spent her afternoon. Nicholas had to admit that he quite enjoyed these highly-coloured accounts of Morna's part in the scourging of the Footers, even though he knew his sister's tendency to exaggerate. Boadicea and Joan of Arc had always been favourites of hers (in fact, in the past she had invented so many games centred on them that Nicholas had frequently had to rebel) and now she obviously saw herself as a real-life combination of them both.

"And I just said, 'Trust me!' and they did," she would declare dramatically, before describing how the Footers had been caught napping in the meadow behind the school; or had been lured into an ambush on the track leading to the squatters' camp.

Inevitably she was beginning to look rather the worse for

wear, with many fine bruises on her arms and legs, Footer-inflicted scratches on her face, and torn hems on at least two dresses. Lucky for her, thought Nicholas, that Aunt Dorothy was such an unobservant person! He could never make up his mind whether Mrs Bugg knew about Morna's warlike activities and kept tactfully silent, or whether she was so preoccupied with worrying about Simon that she did not notice what was going on around her.

Nevertheless, on the morning of Thursday, June the twenty-seventh, Morna still seemed set for an exhilarating summer of confrontations with Footers. Indeed, as she sat at the breakfast table, she had the faraway look in her eyes that told Nicholas she was planning yet another campaign. Then the door suddenly burst open and Mrs Bugg came panting in.

"There's bin a stabbin', Mrs Buchanan!" she gasped, as she sat down next to Nicholas. "A stabbin' in the village!"

Aunt Dorothy's cup landed heavily on its saucer. "For Heaven's sake!" she exclaimed. "Who?"

"Peter Bugg stab Dave Footer arter the dance las' night in the village hall. Peter's Marcus Bugg's boy (you know, them that live up Rectory Lane . . .) an' Dave's Les Footer's eldest. Reckon neither o' them's an angel. Police are down there now askin' questions."

"Is he dead?" asked Morna, her face suddenly as white as her milk.

"No, my old darlin! He ain't dead," Mrs Bugg assured her, leaning over to pat her hand. "That were jest a flesh-wound an' he'll be outa hospital in a week. Still," she went on tremulously, "that's a terrible thing for the village jes' the same. That'll be in the papers, an' what'll folks think? What'll they think when I says my name's Bugg an' I lives in Saxford? 'Huh! One o' them savages!' they'll say to theirselves. That's whoolly upset me, Mrs Buchanan! That really has!"

"I don't wonder," said Aunt Dorothy. "An attempted murder—for that's what it is—almost on our doorstep! It's enough to shock anyone! Morna," she added, frowning, "I'd rather you didn't play down in the village in the meantime.

You can walk to the shops and back, but you must play up here."

"But I have to see Louie . . ." Morna started in dismay.

"Louie can play up here, too," Aunt Dorothy said quickly. "That's if she'd like to, of course!"

"Oh, she'll like to!" Mrs Bugg declared, laughing wheezily. "She think the sun never set on her Morna! She'll be up here like lightnin' when I tells her."

"Fine!" said Aunt Dorothy, looking relieved. Then her eye fell on Nicholas. "I'll be happier about you, too, young man, knowing you have someone to play with," she added. "You'll have to give your old Victor his marching orders and set about organizing Morna and Louie."

Once again Nicholas froze before he realized that, of course, Aunt Dorothy was referring to the imaginary Victor. When he had recovered himself he stared hard at Morna.

"I expect they'll only want to play girls' stupid games," he said provocatively.

"Not stupid enough for you by a long chalk!" Morna retorted, scowling. "So don't expect us to ask you to play."

"I won't," promised Nicholas with a smirk. He could see that he was annoying his aunt, but it could not be helped. To safeguard Victor he would have to keep Morna and Louie at a distance.

"I do wish you would try to be more sociable, Nicholas!" Aunt Dorothy said wearily, as she moved towards the door.

"He's jes' like my Simon," observed Mrs Bugg, starting on the washing-up. "Only happy on his own. There's no changin' them, Mrs Buchanan!"

Nicholas put his elbows on the table so that his fists were over his ears. He wished that they would all stop talking so that he could think. Where would the girls play, he wondered. In the orchard? In his and Morna's room? Should he try to train Victor to come out in the mornings instead of the afternoons? He might do if he only knew where the rat had its home. The trouble was he had no time to take precautions now! Louie would be here this afternoon. Still . . . Victor would keep out of the way if he heard strangers about.

"Nick!" His wrists were seized roughly, and Morna's voice, brassy with exasperation, blared in his ear. "Stop playing the fool!"

"I was only trying to hear myself think!" he objected, pulling away from her. He saw that Aunt Dorothy had departed for her study.

"Then think about your lunch!" Morna ordered him. "We can choose what we want at the butcher's. Mince or lamb-chops. Which is it to be?"

"Chops," he decided.

"Good," she said. "That's what I want." Then she steered him out of the kitchen into the living-room. "Let's hurry!" she whispered. "We might be in time to see the blood."

"But there's always blood in the butcher's," Nicholas said, mystified. "We can't very well miss it."

"Not that blood, stupid! Dave Footer's blood! Outside the village hall. They might not have cleaned it up yet."

"I'd rather just go straight to the butcher's," Nicholas said after a moment.

"You're not frightened?" Morna asked scathingly.

"No," Nicholas told her. "But I haven't got time for that sort of nonsense. I've more important things to think about."

"Like your stupid Victor, I suppose."

"That's right." Nicholas could not hide a smile at the way he was leading Morna up the garden path.

"I think you've gone batty!" Morna declared, staring at him in feigned alarm, as she went off to their room to fetch her skipping-rope. "Perhaps that runs in the Taylor family, too!" she called over her shoulder.

15

Evacuation Plans

"A rat! A rat, Morna! I jes' seen a rat!"

Nicholas, who had been standing moodily by the bedroom window watching Morna search frantically through the cupboard for her lost tennis ball, felt his knees give, and moved over to sit down heavily on his bed. It was Louie Bugg who had shouted. She had arrived only a few minutes ago and was now in the bathroom.

"A rat! Where?" Morna called, abandoning her search for the ball immediately.

Louie erupted from the bathroom. "I were stood on the seat havin' a look at that system–thing, as I ain't hardly never seen one . . ." she started.

"Cistern," Morna corrected her quickly.

"Yes . . . Well, I jes' happen to glance outa that little top window into the yard, an' I see a rat!"

Aunt Dorothy looked in from the lobby. "Did I hear you say you'd seen a rat, Louie?" she asked sharply.

"Yes, Mrs Buchanan. Jes' now. Runnin' about in the yard."

"I've seen that," Nicholas cried, coming out of shock at last. "It's grey, isn't it?"

"That's right," Louie agreed.

"Then it's a mouse," Nicholas said, trying to keep his voice steady and convincing. "It's just a big, grey mouse, Aunt Dorothy. I've seen it once or twice."

"That's never a mouse!" exclaimed Louie scornfully. "That's a little, young rat."

"But I thought rats were mostly brown or sometimes black," Morna put in. "That's what it said at the exhibition."

"Not when they're little 'uns," said Louie. "When they're little 'uns they're grey, an' they turn brown later."

"It's a mouse, I tell you!" insisted Nicholas desperately.

"Oh, dear!" sighed Aunt Dorothy in exasperation. "I

71

suppose I'll have to take the time to look. And I'm just in the middle of a very complicated paragraph!"

"I shouldn't bother, Aunt Dorothy," Nicholas said. "I'm sure it's a mouse. And it will run away when it hears us coming, so there's no point in going round to look."

"That's a rat," Louie muttered. "You ain't never seen a rat, little 'un. You don't know."

"Anyway, we don't actually have to see the rat or the mouse, Nick," Morna pointed out. "We can look for its droppings, like we were shown in those big photographs."

"Yes," agreed Aunt Dorothy. "Let's get it over with. Four pairs of eyes should be able to find something!"

"Five," giggled Louie, giving Nicholas a nudge.

Nicholas could not have smiled back even had he wanted to. He marched grimly out behind the others making as much noise as possible, bumping against the dustbin and kicking stones along the path, so that if Victor were still about, he would take cover.

"Well, whatever it was, it's gone," announced Morna, who liked stating the obvious.

Nicholas walked over towards the stable door, raking the cobbles with narrowed eyes in the hope of kicking any droppings out of sight before the others saw them. Louie followed him.

"It were just about here when I seen it," she said thoughtfully. "Reckon it might've come outa the stable!"

She pulled the stable door open and went inside, then almost immediately called, "Mrs Buchanan! Here! Quickly!"

Nicholas's heart contracted as his aunt hurried past him, and a moment later he knew that he had been right to fear the worst for Aunt Dorothy came out of the stable nodding her head grimly.

"Yes," she announced. "Louie was right. We have a rat, I'm afraid. I'll have to send for the rodent-man."

"Grim-fizz'll 'phone for you, if we ask him, Mrs Buchanan," Louie told her. "He do that for anyone that see a rat. An' the council man'll come out tomorrer mos' likely.

72

You want to get rid of that little varmint right quick, else it'll breed."

"Oh, don't!" begged Aunt Dorothy. "The very thought makes me shudder. Run down to Mr Grimes right away, Morna," she went on, fishing in the pocket of her dress, and handing her a shilling. "Pay him for the 'phone call, and you can buy yourselves some liquorice at Mrs Nelson's with what's left over. There should be plenty for three there."

"I don't want to go," said Nicholas quickly. "Morna and Louie can have my share."

"There won't be no fightin' today, little 'un," said Louie kindly. "Spikey's to stay home 'cos of his brother."

"I don't want to come anyway," said Nicholas, his voice trembling with anxiety in case he would not be allowed to stay behind.

"Then you needn't," said Aunt Dorothy, ruffling his hair. "I'll leave one of Mrs Bugg's doughnuts on the kitchen table for you. That'll make up for the liquorice."

"He's going to play with Brother Victor," Morna teased, as she and Louie headed for the gate. "Give him our love, Nick!"

When Aunt Dorothy had gone in, Nicholas ran out on to the road to gaze after his sister. For a moment he had an overpowering urge to call her back and tell her about Victor. She was the one with the brains and the imagination to hatch plans. She was the one with the boldness to carry them out. Had she been the one to find Victor, she would be thinking right now of some way of saving him from the man with the stick and the poison. She would sit down, scowling, and chewing the end of her pencil, and in five minutes she would come up with a solution.

Well, I'll just have to do the same, he thought, as he turned away and went indoors. I'm as good as she is, really. Look how I went into that bunker on my own! The memory of the colonel's bunker with its musty, silent blackness made him pause halfway along the lobby. If anyone were looking for a hideaway . . . But how could he possibly take the rat down there? Victor was certainly not tame enough to be handled yet.

73

And, anyway, he dare not risk a fatal infection from a rat bite. The visit to the exhibition had taught him that. If there were only something he could carry Victor in! Something unchewable. Something . . .

The answer slid into his head with such suddenness that it startled him. The vase! Why not? Stick the plug in at the end of the vase while Victor was inside it and he could be carried with no difficulty. There were even air-holes along the top, so that he wouldn't suffocate. He leaned against the wall at the end of the lobby, pressing his fingertips against his temples, as though trying to urge his brain to work to greater effect. He longed to rush out that very moment, lure Victor into the vase, and carry him off to safety. As one problem was rooted out, it seemed that another grew in its place, though. For what would he do with Victor once he had him in the bunker? If he freed him, he would probably just make his way back to his old haunts. Yet he could not keep him in the vase. That would be cruel. He needed a kind of cage. A cage . . .

Nicholas pushed open the door of the junk room and ran over to the old bird cage which lay on its side in the centre of the floor. Kneeling down, he righted it. Yes. The door was secure enough, and the bars were too narrowly spaced for Victor to wriggle through. It was a bit rusty, but seemed solid enough with its two metal floors connected by a little ladder. As he stared at it, his mind clicked over. Water dish. Food dish. Pile of bedding. There was plenty of space for what Victor would need. And surely it would be better for him to be caged for a while than poisoned!

The thought of the poison was like a needle-jab. Nicholas jumped up. There was no time to lose. Victor had to be caught while the girls were out of the way. Caught. And carried down to the bunker. He could leave him there in the vase while he came back and arranged the cage. But the rescue must be carried out immediately.

He darted across to his room to fish his torch out from under his pillow and stuck it in his trouser pocket. Then he hurried through to the kitchen to break off a piece of the doughnut

74

Aunt Dorothy had left out for him. Thus armed, he ran round to the yard. He stored Victor's playthings just inside the stable door, and as he lifted the vase his eyes fell on Simon Bugg's gardening gloves. He picked them up and put them on. They were sizes too big for him, but he could still use his hands effectively, and it was best to be on the safe side, he told himself. He pulled the vase's stopper out and dropped the piece of doughnut in before placing the vase on the cobbles. Then he retreated a few paces and waited.

Precious minutes passed with no sign of Victor. Nicholas's palms grew damp inside the thick gloves. The rat had been frightened off, he decided dismally. He would not come back again this afternoon. Now there would be no opportunity to rescue him before the rat-catcher came with his poison. Then, just as the last trickle of hope oozed away, Nicholas looked up and there was Victor, nose twitching energetically as he caught the whiff of doughnut.

Creeping on his belly, Victor approached the vase. Oddly enough, for the first time ever, he seemed wary of it as though he sensed a trap. It was probably because there had never been food in it before, Nicholas thought. Suddenly making up his mind, he raced straight for it and disappeared inside. Nicholas had to move as quickly, banging his knees on the ground as he dived over to press in the vase's stopper. Immediately Victor set up a frantic scrabbling. The vase would have rolled over and over had Nicholas not picked it up.

"It's all right," he called softly through the holes. "It's going to be all right, Victor! Calm down!"

Then cradling the vase in the crook of his arm, he ran through the orchard as fast as he could go, darting nervous glances over his shoulder, but happily seeing no one.

16

Mission Accomplished

The front of the bunker, which had seemed as large as Gramarye's drawing room when Nicholas had groped his way around it in the dark, revealed itself in the torchlight as being only about eight foot square, brick-lined, and with a door in the back wall. Nicholas choked as the mustiness caught at his throat; then, after a moment's hesitation, he walked across and pushed open the door. The second compartment was smaller, but equally bare, with a round hole in the centre of the ceiling which was obviously the end of a ventilation shaft.

"You'll be all right here. It'll be just like the inside of your burrow," Nicholas murmured to Victor whose scrabblings had by now diminished to an occasional half-hearted thumping. "And once you're in your cage, you'll be very comfortable," he added reassuringly.

He placed the vase gently on the earthen floor, closing the door behind him as he left. Once outside the bunker he set off at a fast trot, thinking of all he had to do before the girls arrived back. He could use the old, glass ashtray from the junk room as a water dish. But what could he put Victor's food in? He knew the shape and the size of the container that he wanted. An image floated up. That was it! The iron dolls' bath that Gramarye had once given Morna, and which had only ever been used for the zoo-animals because it was too small for the dolls. It was at the bottom of the cupboard, in the back right-hand corner. She would never miss it.

He had to find something for Victor to nest in, too. Something soft yet bulky, like cottonwool, or the kapok with which Nooka was stuffed, and which occasionally burst through his skin. As his sandals flicked up the dust at the edge of the wheat field, Nicholas tried to chase away the dark thought that had suddenly leaped into his head. No! He could not bear to do that! Not to Nooka who had been his inseparable companion for as long as he could remember! One-eared now, and with bare patches all over him, he was still a powerful support in any uncomfortable situation. And yet . . .

By the time Nicholas staggered panting through the back door and into the empty kitchen, he had determined Nooka's fate. He lifted the scissors from their hook above the copper and hurred to the bedroom to do what was necessary. When he carried the kapok through to the junk room he found that he had enough to fill the entire top shelf of the cage. Then he placed the ashtray and the bath on the cage-bottom and stood back. It was just as he had envisaged it. Victor could live there, if not happily, at least comfortably. All that was needed now was food and water.

He found a small carrot in the bottom tray of the vegetable rack in the kitchen and chopped it up on a plate with trembling fingers. He was terrified that the girls would burst in on him. If they did, he decided, he would just have to pretend he was making himself an odd kind of beevers. He added a small handful of cornflakes and the crumbled-up heel of a loaf, and hurried through to transfer the lot from the plate into the dolls' bath. He did not know how much one small rat would eat in a day, but since he was now Victor's only source of food, he knew he would have to give him more than the scraps he had thrown to him in the yard.

He decided in the end to carry the water down to the bunker in the small brandy bottle which had been Bridget's, and which he and Morna used as a face-warmer if they had tooth-ache. He found it where he had seen Morna put it: on the top shelf of the bathroom cabinet.

And now, if the coast's clear, I can go, he thought.

He tiptoed through to the kitchen holding the cage behind his back. The pulse in his temple was throbbing and his mouth was so dry that he felt faintly sick. If they see me I'll pretend I'm going to try to catch a bird, he decided. They'll probably believe me. Girls think boys are stupid enough for anything! There was still no sign of Morna and Louie, though, and as he climbed the fence at the foot of the orchard, Nicholas blessed whoever, or whatever, had detained them. Perhaps Morna was telling Grim-fizz her life story. Or perhaps Grim-fizz was telling Morna and Louie about rats. On the other hand there might just have been a crowd in Mrs Nelson's when the girls went in to buy their liquorice.

Thinking of his sister and trying to imagine what she was doing had a peculiar effect on Nicholas. It brought him to an abrupt halt halfway along the wheat-field path. There he stood, gazing across the wide green sea of young wheat, then upwards at the high blank sky, and a wave of frightening loneliness engulfed him. When it receded he was left stranded, a minute speck between the green disc and the grey one. What was he doing, running away from Morna like this, he asked himself. Why had he not stuck beside her and put up with the Buggs and the fighting? At least he would have been with people, and everything would have been warm and noisy.

Then he looked down at the cage and remembered all he had accomplished in the past hour-and-a-half. On his own, without help from anyone, he had thought up these ideas and made them work. Victor was safe. Soon he would be comfortable, too. And it was all his doing! The sense of his responsibility for Victor heated his blood again. The chill went out of him. Lark song dropped around him like warm rain. A tall, creamy-headed flower wafted its perfume towards him from beneath the hedge. He began to run, holding the cage level so that the food would not spill out over the floor. He pushed it carefully ahead of him through the hedge, and almost bent himself in two avoiding the barbed wire, as he lowered it over the gate. He arrived with it intact, gasping for breath as he stumbled, by the light of his small torch, into the bunker's inner compartment.

The vase lay where he had left it, but there was neither sound nor movement from it now. A cold band tightened round Nicholas's chest as he looked down at it. Those holes in the top of the vase . . . surely they would let in enough air! Surely . . .

He knelt down quickly, placing the cage and the torch on the floor. Opening the cage door, he filled the ashtray with water from his bottle, spilling a little, because he was wearing Simon's gloves again and his fingers moved clumsily. Then, trying to control the shaking of his hands, he removed the stopper from the vase and deftly inserted the open end into the cage. There was a scuffle, followed by a soft 'plop', and Victor sat looking at him with pin-sharp eyes. Nicholas's breath came out in a long hiss of relief as he withdrew the vase and closed the cage door.

"There!" he said in a shaky voice. "What do you think of your new home, Victor?"

For answer the rat began to scrabble frantically at the metal floor of the cage, his front feet working faster and faster as he tried to burrow his way to freedom. He was still digging fifteen minutes later when Nicholas finally left him.

"He'll settle down when he notices his food and finds his nest," he told himself, screwing his eyes against the daylight as he came out of the bunker. "At least I hope he will!"

What if he doesn't, though, a morbid voice inside his head nagged. What if he batters himself to death against the bars? What if he dies of exhaustion trying to dig his way out? How will you feel then?

So preoccupied was Nicholas in fighting off these dark imaginings that he did not notice the figure who had been standing, motionless, at the end of the cutting, and who slipped quickly back into the bushes as Nicholas started towards him.

"Nicholas! You look exhausted!" Aunt Dorothy observed in some alarm at teatime. "Are you feeling all right?"

"Yes, thank you," he replied quietly.

Morna leaned forward to peer at him. "I should think he's sickening for something," she said cheerfully. "That was how he looked before he caught measles and chickenpox . . . I hope it's not scarlet fever. That can be deadly."

"Perhaps you and Louie had better keep away from me, just in case," Nicholas said quickly, remembering how difficult it was going to be to escape the girls when he wanted to visit Victor.

"So you do feel a little bit poorly?" Aunt Dorothy asked sharply.

"Just very tired," Nicholas admitted.

"Run along, then! Early bed, Sir Nicholas. No washing up for you tonight," Aunt Dorothy said firmly as she rose to clear the table. "We don't want you falling asleep helping to dry."

"No!" Morna agreed with feeling.

"I'm not a baby . . ." Nicholas was starting indignantly, when Aunt Dorothy let out a puzzled, "Oh!" She was staring into the breadbin.

"What is it?" Morna asked.

"There was an old, leathery heel of a loaf I was going to use for fish-crumbs," she said. "And it seems to have vanished . . . I don't imagine either of you two was ravenous enough to eat it?"

"I didn't," replied Morna. "And you know how Nick hates crusts, so he certainly wouldn't eat a heel!"

"No. That's what I was thinking," said Aunt Dorothy, frowning.

Nicholas, ready to drop with fatigue, was feeling altogether too weak to deal with the prickings of conscience that were beginning to assail him. He sidled towards the door, wished his aunt and Morna a hasty goodnight, then bolted for bed.

17

Strange Encounter

"Seems there's only one of them. So that's a good thing," Mr Bullace, the rat-catcher, observed, pushing his floppy-brimmed hat further back on his head.

He had arrived while they were having breakfast, and now they were following him round the yard while he did his

80

detective work, bending occasionally to peer intently at the ground. Opening the stable door he gave a succession of satisfied grunts and, when he finally turned round, his brick-red face was beaming.

"We'll get the little varmint for sure, do I lay my stuff here," he announced. "This is where he feed. Reckon he musta lost his family to one of the farm cats, an' he's been a-wanderin'."

"Isn't he very old, then?" asked Nicholas tightly.

"I'd guess no more than five weeks," replied Mr Bullace. "Rats grow up quicker nor boys. An' they're a darned sight cleverer too, on the whole," he finished with a sly wink at Morna, who gave her rippling laugh.

"Where will you put the poison?" asked Aunt Dorothy, glancing down uneasily at Mr Bullace's bucket of creamy liquid.

The rat-catcher walked to the back of the stable where the paraffin was stored. "That's been here arter some old rotten apples," he called, "so I'll lay my stuff under those. Don't none of you touch it now," he added jocularly. "Don't want to hev to carry boys nor gels in my sack, 'stead of old, dead rats!"

Morna shrieked, pretending to be terrified, and scurried away across the yard.

"How long will the poison take to work?" Aunt Dorothy asked when Mr Bullace finally emerged from the stable.

"I'll be back next Friday—a week from today," he told her. "The little varmint should've give up the ghost by then. Happen you see it wanderin' in the yard, very slow an' staggery, jes' you ignore it, Missus. That'll creep off in a corner somewheres to die."

"Look at Nick's face!" Morna exclaimed, all at once. "It's giving him away. I don't think he wants the horrid old rat to be caught!"

"Of course he does!" Aunt Dorothy said sharply. "It's just the thought of how it's done that's not very pleasant."

"Don't you go wastin' no sympathy on rats, bor!" Mr Bullace told Nicholas sternly. "Them's nasty, filthy, cunnin', little varmints, an' that's either them or mankind on this earth.

81

The only good rat's a dead 'un. Take it from me!"

"Yes," mumbled Nicholas.

He was hot with embarrassment and guilt. Mr Bullace made him feel like a criminal or a traitor. Was he a traitor to mankind because he was sheltering one small rat? Mr Bullace would certainly think he was. And he suspected that Aunt Dorothy, Morna, and many other people might think so too. He could imagine the words they would use about him if they knew what he had done. Stupid. Irresponsible. Evil. 'As evil as Hitler,' they might say. That would be terrible.

"Nick!" Morna was shouting, poking him between the shoulder-blades. "Mr Bullace is saying goodbye to you!"

"Goodbye!" said Nicholas mechanically, starting out of his reverie.

"He's dreamin' about his best gel, I reckon!" Mr Bullace called, giving Nicholas a cheerful wave before climbing into his van.

"Dreaming about Victor more likely," remarked Morna with a condescending smile.

"Dreaming, anyway! And not very happy," said Aunt Dorothy, frowning down at Nicholas. "I think I'll go with Morna for the shopping this morning and give you a rest. You still look tired, young man."

Immediately Nicholas stopped feeling guilty and uncomfortable, and began to feel excited and cheerful, since he realized he would now be able to visit Victor within the next hour instead of waiting until the afternoon. He had been worrying about him ever since he had left him trying to dig up the floor of his cage. The worry had been like a toothache, sometimes sharp, sometimes dull, but it had never left him.

Then Morna almost ruined everything.

"I wouldn't be surprised if he had a temperature," she said, staring at him. "Look how red his cheeks are! Perhaps he ought to go back to bed."

"Don't be stupid!" said Nicholas furiously. "I'm only red because I got embarrassed."

"Why?"

"Because of Mr Bullace."

"Why? Not because he said you had a best girl, you idiot?"

"Maybe . . . Anyway, it's none of your business!"

"Oh, you two!" exclaimed Aunt Dorothy. "I'll be the one with a temperature if you don't stop bickering. Come along, Morna! Leave Nicholas alone!"

"With pleasure!" said Morna stonily, stalking on ahead into the kitchen to collect the shopping bags.

As soon as his aunt and Morna had gone, Nicholas sprang into action. Mrs Bugg was not due until after lunch today, so he had the cottage to himself. He cut a slice from the loaf, took an apple from the fruit bowl on the dresser, then filled the brandy bottle with water and stuffed the lot into one pocket. After that he went round to the stable to find a small piece of wood for Victor to gnaw. He shoved this into his other pocket on top of the torch. Then he set off at a run along the familiar route to the bunker.

By now he had become so hardened a trespasser that it gave him hardly a qualm to squeeze through the gate, dodging the barbed wire. Indeed he had almost forgotten Colonel Cutworth's existence as he ran on to the opening of the bunker. Once there, however, he stopped, suddenly afraid to go in. What if Victor had died in the night? What if he had killed the rat by imprisoning it? A lump came into his throat as he imagined the small, grey body lying stretched out on the floor of the cage.

Then he took a grip of himself, switched on the torch and marched resolutely to the inner door. As he opened it, he heard an alarmed scuffle and gave a sigh of relief. At least Victor was still alive! He knelt down to look in the cage. There was no sign of the rat, though half the food had been eaten, and most of the water was gone. Then he saw the pile of kapok lift very slightly and settle again. Oh, glory! Victor was in his nest! He had settled in, after all.

Nicholas had left Simon's gloves on the floor beside the cage. Now he quickly put them on and pulled the bottle of water from his pocket so that he could fill the water dish while

Victor was hiding. He opened the cage door, poured the water into the dish, and pulled his hand out again. Not a tremor from the kapok! He fumbled the piece of wood out of his pocket, dropped that on the cage floor, then closed the door.

"Victor! Victor!" he called softly.

The cage might have been empty.

"Victor!"

Not a sound.

This is going to be dreary, Nicholas thought. And not much good, if I want to tame him. Perhaps if I took him outside into the sunshine . . .

He lifted the cage and carried it carefully through the doorway and across the outer room. As he set it down on the grass, Victor's head popped out briefly, then disappeared. Nicholas took the apple from his pocket, bit a piece off, then shoved it through the bars. After a moment Victor's head emerged again, then his forelegs. Nose twitching, he began to come down the ladder, making his body long—wriggling down in little, snake-like jerks. When he reached the floor he picked up the apple and went off to the corner to eat it, turning his back on Nicholas.

Nicholas repeated the performance until half the apple was gone. He decided to keep the remaining half to put into the cage with the bread, before he left. Victor found the wood and began to gnaw at it busily. He certainly did not seem to be pining in captivity, Nicholas observed with satisfaction. In fact he could almost have imagined that the rat had grown a little since yesterday. He was on his knees, face close to the cage, studying Victor, when the rat suddenly panicked, dropped the wood, and leaped up the ladder and into the kapok.

"Silly!" Nicholas grumbled.

A shadow fell diagonally across the cage. Nicholas's stomach turned over and his knees refused to support him so that he sank down on to his heels. He dared not look up. Had he been caught by the colonel himself? Or by one of his keepers? Would he be arrested? If he were arrested, would he be tried both for trespassing and for keeping a wild rat? What-

84

ever would Morna say? The questions scurried round his brain like leaves caught up in a whirlwind. Was the shadow never going to speak?

"That's a baby rat, bor! Did you know that?" a hoarse voice asked at last.

Nicholas was pretty sure that the broad Suffolk accent could not belong to the colonel, and he felt a little more hopeful. A gamekeeper might be more lenient. He turned his head slowly and found himself looking up at an unshaven, gaunt man, wearing rumpled, grass-stained dungarees. "That's a rat," Simon Bugg repeated in his flat voice.

"I know," said Nicholas shakily, feeling as afraid now as though it *had* been the colonel standing there. Simon was such a strange person. And, apart from that, it was somehow alarming to hear a voice come out of him at last. He felt that the peculiar, hoarse voice might begin to say awful things. And here he was, trapped between it and the bunker.

Simon remained silent, though, staring down at his gloves, which Nicholas still wore.

"I'm trying to tame him," Nicholas started, launching into a desperate and disjointed explanation. "I thought I could have him disinfected. His name's Victor, because of the 'V' on his back. I borrowed your gloves in case he bit me. I hope you don't mind. I brought him here because they were going to poison him. You can see how intelligent he is. He's learned all about his cage in just one night. I expect he'll become tame very quickly."

He ran out of breath, then waited for Simon to tell him what a wicked boy he was, and how he would have to report to Aunt Dorothy what he had done. All Simon did say, however, after a long silence, was, "I don't want no one knowin' I'm down here. Understand? No one!"

"I won't tell a soul!" Nicholas promised fervently, and crossed his heart with the waggling finger of Simon's glove.

Simon nodded slowly, then turned and walked away to disappear into the bushes at the end of the cutting.

Nicholas let out a sigh of profound relief as he picked up the cage and carried it back into the bunker. He dropped in the apple and the bread, before removing the gloves and putting them on the floor.

" 'Bye, Victor!" he muttered. "See you tomorrow!"

As he said it, he realized that he would have to see Victor on every single tomorrow from now on, otherwise the rat might die of hunger or thirst. This suddenly seemed a grave and daunting responsibility.

It also struck him that whenever he came to the bunker, he ran the risk of meeting Simon Bugg. This was not a pleasant thought either, for Simon, with his strange manner, made him feel uneasy and sometimes positively afraid.

So although he could not help but be pleased with himself for having carried out Victor's evacuation so capably, it was with mixed feelings that he started on his way home.

Later that afternoon he found himself in another uncomfortable situation. He had been playing an unexciting game of hide-and-seek with Morna and Louie so had not been sorry when Mrs Bugg's summons to beevers had brought it to an end. As soon as he walked into the kitchen though, ahead of the others, he could see from Mrs Bugg's red eyes that she had been crying again.

"Are you upset, Mrs Bugg?" he asked hesitantly as he sat down. He was not sure whether it would have been more polite to have pretended that he had noticed nothing.

Mrs Bugg seemed grateful for his interest. She gave him a watery smile.

"Jes' the same old trouble, my love," she replied in a thick voice. "Jes' worritin' about that boy o' mine. Dreamed he were drowned las' night, an' that keep comin' back into my head."

"Oh, I'm sure he's not, Mrs Bugg!" Nicholas cried in dismay.

If only he could have told her that he had seen Simon that morning! She was such a kind, good woman. She did not deserve to be made miserable for no reason.

But he had given his word. And a Newton must never go back on his word. How often had Morna drilled that into him?

86

So all he could finally offer in the way of comfort was to help with the washing up which he felt was not very satisfactory— either to Mrs Bugg or to himself.

When later he went out again he stood glaring resentfully down the orchard at Morna, who was trying to play leapfrog with Louie and kept tumbling over and shrieking with laughter. It seemed very unfair that she should be so lighthearted when all these cares had somehow crept up on him! After all, if she had not deserted him in the first place . . .

He suddenly became aware of Louie waving her arms to attract his attention. "Come on, little 'un!" she called. "Come you here an' make a back, so's I can show Morna what to do."

Nicholas hesitated for a moment, then with a long-suffering sigh plodded down to join the girls.

18

The Millstone

As soon as he woke on Sunday morning Nicholas told Morna that he did not want to go on the picnic which Aunt Dorothy had planned for that afternoon.

"You're turning very odd, you know," Morna observed crisply. "If you don't watch out you'll grow up like Mr Butterworth."

"No, I won't!" said Nicholas, sitting straight up in bed to glare at his sister.

Mr Butterworth was a very eccentric old gentleman with a house at the end of Gramarye's avenue who shuffled back and forth from the shops in his carpet slippers and a mildewy top-hat.

"You will," said Morna remorselessly, as she settled Anastasia in a more graceful position on the pillow beside her. "You're turning odder and odder. Look how you've hidden Nooka away. And look what you did to my books!"

"You deserved what I did to your books," said Nicholas sulkily. "You betrayed me."

Morna gave him a single, exasperated look, then changed her tactics. "You'll love a picnic anyway," she said cajolingly. "You've never been on a proper picnic before, Nick. Only on those silly pretend ones with Bridget in the park. It's very kind of Aunt Dorothy to think of it; and to use her petrol. She'll be very hurt if you say you don't want to go . . . I will too," she added as an afterthought.

"No, you won't," said Nicholas tightly. "You'll have Louie. You won't even notice I'm not there."

"Well, Aunt Dorothy will," observed Morna, reverting to her former sharpness. "She might even cancel the picnic. That's what's really worrying me."

"I thought it might be," Nicholas sneered.

"And if she does I'll never speak to you again," said Morna grimly. "Not even when you're having a nightmare!"

Nicholas gave a bitter little laugh. Much Morna knew about him nowadays!

"Anyway," Morna finished, "Aunt Dorothy will make you go."

"She can't," said Nicholas. "Not if I say that I feel terribly tired, and my legs ache."

He jumped out of bed and ran into the bathroom so that Morna would not see how perturbed he was. He was in a predicament. Last night, just before they went to bed, Aunt Dorothy had announced that Sunday was to be a busy day. In the morning they were to help her weed the vegetable garden, and in the afternoon, as a reward, she was going to drive them out to have a picnic. ("And, yes! Louie can come," she had added, as Morna had opened her mouth to ask.)

Nicholas had been appalled. How was he ever going to escape to attend to Victor he wondered. He could not possibly miss a day. It was not food but water that was the problem. The rat's water dish had been empty by the time he had managed to elude Morna and Louie on Saturday afternoon. No doubt it would have drunk it dry again in another twenty-four hours. Before he fell asleep he had decided that the only solution was for him to insist on staying at home while the others went off on their picnic. Now, it appeared that this was not going to be as simple as he had imagined.

As he brushed his teeth, scowling at himself in the mirror, he tried to think of how best to act. It was like playing Morna's war-games. He needed strategy. He had been a fool to blurt out his intentions to his sister. He would have to try to convince her now that he had changed his mind, or she would go and blab to Aunt Dorothy, and she must not know until the very last minute that he did not want to go with them, otherwise she might indeed cancel the picnic which would not suit him at all!

"Perhaps I will come on the picnic after all," he remarked casually, five minutes later, as he finished dressing.

Morna was brushing her hair, making it smooth for Aunt Dorothy to plait.

"I knew you would," she said, flashing him an approving smile over her shoulder. "You don't really like upsetting people, do you?"

"No," Nicholas replied truthfully.

This was very evident at three o'clock that afternoon when he stood in the living room, his flushed face puckered unhappily, and said for the second time (Aunt Dorothy had just asked him to repeat it), "I don't feel like coming for a picnic. I feel very tired, and my legs ache."

Morna threw him a baleful look, took Louie's arm, and stood gazing apprehensively at Aunt Dorothy.

"That don't mean *we* can't go, do it, Mrs Buchanan?" Louie burst out, unable to contain her concern. She had on her rose-patterned dress, and there was a strong smell of shoe polish from her worn, red sandals.

"Well, it depends," said Aunt Dorothy, beginning to look flustered. "If Nicholas is feeling ill, I can't very well leave him."

"Oh, I don't feel properly ill," Nicholas assured her. "Not sick or anything. I'd just like to lie down and rest my legs."

"That'll be growin' pains," said Louie knowingly. "I had growin' pains. An' so did my sister what's in America. Those ain't serious, though."

"Yes," Nicholas agreed, grateful for support from this unexpected quarter. "I think that's what it must be. I'll be quite all right on my own, Aunt Dorothy."

"He will," Morna put in sourly. "He would tell us if he felt ill. He's not at all brave."

"Well, if you won't come, that's that!" said Aunt Dorothy, beginning to sound more displeased than anxious now. "Not that I understand you. At your age I wouldn't have missed a picnic for anything!"

"Mam says he's like our Simon," Louie observed with a tolerant smile. "Don't like company. Leastways not human company."

Nicholas gave an embarrassed little laugh, then made an awkward exit, tripping over his own feet at the door because everyone was looking at him. He was glad to reach the quiet bedroom where he could sit down and listen for the others' leaving. The cruel part was that he would have loved dearly to have gone on the picnic; especially in Aunt Dorothy's car and with a proper picnic-hamper just like Ratty's in *The Wind in the Willows*. He was making a great sacrifice for Victor's sake and no one knew it. Instead of people seeing how kind he was, they thought he was peculiar and a pest. It really was most unfair!

When he arrived at the bunker twenty minutes later, however, and found that Victor's water dish was indeed empty, and that he had hardly any food left, he could only feel relieved that he had come. He had brought some more dried peas (having discovered by chance the day before that Victor was extremely fond of them), and it was while he was emptying these into Victor's dish that the rat gave him a scare. Up until now Victor had always remained in his nest while Nicholas was refilling his dishes. But today for some reason (perhaps the smell of his favourite food made him savage), he came slithering down the ladder to sink his sharp teeth into the little finger

90

of Simon Bugg's glove. The glove being so large, Victor missed Nicholas's finger. Nevertheless Nicholas pulled his hand out of the cage in a panic.

"What d'you do that for?" he shouted.

Victor ignored him and dived into the peas.

At the same time the torch, which was lying on the floor, began to flicker ominously. "Oh, no!" Nicholas groaned. The battery was fading. He picked the cage up hurriedly and carried it out into the open, switching the torch off as soon as he could. It had not occurred to him that he must be using the battery up fairly quickly. How would he explain that to Aunt Dorothy? And he would have to. For he would never manage in the bunker without a torch.

Then, as though this problem were not enough, he found another one confronting him when he looked down into the cage sitting at his feet. The floor of it was littered with droppings! He had not noticed the mess yesterday because he had been nervous of meeting Simon again, and had not brought the cage out into the daylight. He would have to clear it out soon. But how? At the moment he just could not imagine!

"V for Victor . . . Dot, dot, dash", he chanted morosely, as he lay on his back beside the cage and stared up at the fragments of sky he could see amongst the leaves and branches. They were like the shapes in his kaleidoscope, except that they were all eggshell-blue and not different colours. Busy, contented rat noises came from Victor as he ate his peas, ground his new block of wood into sawdust, scuttled up and down his ladder, and made an occasional, half-hearted attempt to dig through the floor. These sounds gradually soothed Nicholas. The feeling of being harassed and beset by problems faded, to be replaced by a comfortable satisfaction at what he had achieved for Victor. Soon the satisfaction swelled into a rosy optimism about the future. He pictured himself at some not-too-distant date leading Aunt Dorothy and Morna down to the bunker to show them a Victor who would respond to a whistle, roll his vase on command, and give other proofs of

91

outstanding intelligence. He imagined Aunt Dorothy readily agreeing that Victor was not an ordinary rat; and that, once disinfected, he could certainly become a family pet. He saw Morna, incredulous and envious, listening to how he had rescued, hidden and tamed the rat.

For a while he lay in a heavy-limbed, comfortable stupor, half day-dreaming, half dozing. Then suddenly he began to feel very hungry, and it dawned on him that he must have been at the bunker for some considerable time. He quickly stowed Victor away, then set off for home at a run. As he slipped through the gate, he happened to turn his head and saw Simon Bugg standing on the track, just beyond the bunker. Nicholas raised his arm in an uncertain wave, but Simon made no response, quickly turning his back and striding away.

Nicholas was halfway up the orchard before he realized there was trouble in store for him. But as soon as he saw Aunt Dorothy, Morna and Louie standing in a grim-faced line under the kitchen window, he knew he had been caught out.

"And where exactly have you been?" Aunt Dorothy demanded as he approached with faltering steps. Her voice was rasping and unpleasant, not like her normal one at all.

"We've spent two hours looking for you!" Morna exclaimed furiously. "You've wasted our whole afternoon!"

"But I thought you'd gone on a picnic!" Nicholas blurted out.

"We did," said Louie glumly. "Only a wasp come in the car an' give me a dirty great sting. So we come back for the vinegar. Then we couldn't find you nowheres."

"I'm still waiting for an answer, Nicholas Newton!" the new, granite-faced Aunt Dorothy pointed out.

"I was in the field," Nicholas told her, since this was partly true.

"That's a lie! We looked there three times!" Morna cried.

"It's not a lie!"

"It obviously was a lie, though, when you claimed to be tired and have sore legs," Aunt Dorothy said sternly. "That's what makes me really angry. You've been very deceitful,

Nicholas, and have worried me dreadfully. I don't think I want to look at you for a while. Go to your room!"

"He's becoming a millstone round my neck, that boy!" he heard Morna declare dramatically as he shuffled shamefacedly into the kitchen and out of range of their accusing eyes.

She doesn't know what a millstone is, Nicholas thought bitterly. I do, though. I have one. It lives down in Colonel Cutworth's bunker!

19

The Storm

"You oughtn't to go worritin' your aunt, my old darlin'," Mrs Bugg said kindly to Nicholas on Monday morning as he stood in the kitchen waiting for Morna to collect the shopping money from Aunt Dorothy. "Reckon she got enough on her plate, what with your uncle bein' in foreign parts, an' all that paperwork she do. Once she's little 'uns of her own she'll git used to worritin'. But she take it hard at the moment."

"I didn't mean to worry her," said Nicholas, frowning unhappily at the toes of his sandals. Nowadays he seemed to spend his life apologizing or making excuses, he thought ruefully.

"Don't 'spect you did," sighed Mrs Bugg, who was perched on a stool by the sink, cleaning cutlery. "Don't 'spect our Simon mean to be worritin' his poor mother into her grave. That's jes' young folks' nature."

"I'm sure Simon's all right!" Nicholas cried with such fervour that Mrs Bugg turned to stare at him. "It's just a feeling I have," he finished lamely.

"That cheer me up some," Mrs Bugg said, nodding slowly. "I gits feelins too, Nicholas. An' more often than not, there's suffin in 'em."

All morning Nicholas wracked his brains trying to think of

how he could slip away to Victor that afternoon without arousing suspicion. Finally he hit on the idea of writing a letter to Gramarye and asking if he might take it down to the post office. On his way back from the village, he could cut off into the woods and attend briefly to Victor, before continuing on his way home.

"What a sneaky thing to do!" Morna exclaimed indignantly at lunchtime when Nicholas produced his letter and ostentatiously shoved it into an envelope. He had spent the last fifteen minutes writing it in the bathroom so that Morna should not see what he was doing. "You know we always write our letters together!" she went on angrily. "You've probably filled it with fibs."

"I have not!" said Nicholas hotly.

"Enough!" said Aunt Dorothy firmly, pushing the dish of salad towards Morna. "If Nicholas wants to write a private letter, it's no one else's business."

"Well, he needn't expect me to go with him to post it," Morna said huffily.

"I don't," said Nicholas, inwardly jubilant. "I can go on my own."

"I should think you could," agreed Aunt Dorothy, smiling at him. "After all, you are nine years old."

"I could do lots more than he can, when I was nine," Morna pointed out scornfully.

She could not have done this, though, Nicholas thought at three o'clock that afternoon as he deftly poured out Victor's fresh water, then filled the rat's food dish with dried peas and cornflakes. She would have been terrified of Victor for a start. Girls were stupid about that sort of thing!

He had had to take the cage outside again, because of the dying torch, so he could not help but notice that the droppings in the cage had increased. There were damp patches on the bottom floor, too, and the cage was beginning to smell.

"I'll clean out your cage tomorrow," he promised Victor who, fortunately, did not appear to mind the growing squalor of his quarters.

As Nicholas trudged away from the bunker he was already caught up in the next day's problems. What could he use to clean out the cage? How could he prevent Victor from escaping while he was doing it? How could he slip away from the cottage again unnoticed?

"You look like Atlas with the world on his shoulders," Aunt Dorothy observed that evening, looking down on Nicholas, who sat cross-legged on the living room floor, his chin in his hands.

Morna, who had just had her first tiff with Louie in the afternoon, scowled at him briefly.

A gloom seemed to have descended on them all, Nicholas thought, looking round the living room. Even Aunt Dorothy seemed unhappily preoccupied.

The reason for their aunt's worried silence became clear a few minutes later when she suddenly said, "Someone has been taking food from the kitchen!" There was a shocked silence.

"Do you mean that food has been stolen?" Morna asked eventually.

"I suppose that's the correct word for it," Aunt Dorothy replied. She was looking grim. "One has to be so careful about food nowadays that I know exactly what I should have in my larder. I've just been taking stock, and it seems we've lost about four ounces of dried peas, a fair quantity of cornflakes, and some porridge-oats."

"Perhaps it's mice," Nicholas suggested, in a voice that quavered, despite his efforts to steady it. He kept his chin in his hands, so that his guilty, red cheeks were hidden.

"How could mice open a screw-top jar of peas?" Morna demanded impatiently. "And there was the heel of the loaf, that went missing, too, Aunt Dorothy! Don't you remember?" she added excitedly.

"Yes. I remember," Aunt Dorothy said. "I don't suppose either of you has seen anyone?" she asked, looking from one to the other.

Morna and Nicholas shook their heads.

"Perhaps . . ." Morna began.

"Well?"

"You don't think Simon Bugg . . ."

"I did wonder," sighed Aunt Dorothy. "Oh, it's all so unpleasant," she went on unhappily. "I do hate this sort of thing!"

"We could mount a watch," said Morna, her eyes beginning to gleam, "or set traps for them. Sprinkle the jar-lids with flour to catch their fingerprints!"

"Oh, for goodness' sake, Morna! It's not a game. It's serious and very nasty," Aunt Dorothy burst out. Then, glancing at Morna's mortified face, she said hastily, "Oh, I'm sorry, kitten! I'm rather overworked at the moment, I'm afraid. And I do miss your Uncle Robin when all these problems come along . . . Your suggestions were very sensible."

That night Nicholas dreamed he was back in the table-shelter in Gramarye's kitchen, and that he could not open the door to let himself out. He shouted and screamed and flung himself against the sides, but no one paid any attention. Then he noticed that the big kitchen table was spread for a party with sandwiches and cakes and jellies, and that Victor was sitting in the middle of it all. Suddenly he knew that Victor was going to eat everything! First the food. Then the table. Then the kitchen. Then . . .

He began to scream.

"What is it, Nicholas?" Victor asked coldly, turning to stare at him. "What do you want?"

"I want to be free!" he yelled. "Set me free! Please set me free!"

His despairing cries were still echoing in his ears when he was wakened by Morna's rough shaking, and her cross voice complaining bitterly about the noise he was making.

"That's buildin' up for suffin out there!" Mrs Bugg announced when she arrived with Louie just after lunch on Tuesday. "Clouds are really piled up. The old anvil's up in the sky, too. Come you here an' look." She led them to the back door and pointed to a great, triangular mass of dark cloud. "God's anvil,

96

that is. What he make the thunder on," she told them. As though to confirm her words, there was a long low menacing rumble.

"Bes' keep good an' close to the cottage till it go by," she advised them. "An' don't be goin' near no trees, neither, case o' lightnin'."

Morna and Louie, who were best friends again, ran off giggling and chattering to the bedroom. Nicholas remained in the kitchen doorway staring up at the sky. It seemed to darken, even as he looked at it, and the thunder growled again much more loudly.

"That's a–comin'!" Mrs Bugg called warningly.

Nicholas sighed. He had everything prepared to take down to Victor. The water bottle was filled and in his pocket. He had managed to slip some potatoes from his plate at lunchtime into his handkerchief. And he had seen a small, hard brush in the stable, which would be ideal for cleaning out Victor's cage. He could have set off for the bunker right now, had it not been for this stupid storm.

Blue-white zig-zags of lightning flickered over the black cushions of cloud. There was a tremendous crash, under which the cottage seemed to stagger.

"Shut the door!" Mrs Bugg cried in alarm.

As Nicholas did so the hailstorm began. Giant stones bounded from the walls and windows like ricocheting bullets.

Mrs Bugg emitted a single, hoarse "Corblast!" and pointed towards the orchard. Nicholas ran to her side to watch, horrified, as the trees writhed and bowed beneath the bombardment. Leaves, twigs, and finally whole branches fell on to grass already beaten flat and covered by a white carpet of ice.

"Big as walnuts, some o' them stones! Never seen nuffin like that!" Mrs Bugg gasped.

Morna and Louie came shrieking into the living room.

"Come and listen!" Morna commanded exultantly. "Come into the bathroom."

They found Aunt Dorothy already there. She pointed to the window to indicate that the tremendous, incredible sound was made by the hailstones falling on the cobbles of the yard.

Then, gradually, the noise lessened, came in intermittent bursts, then ceased altogether. There was a minute's uneasy silence, before the rain began.

"Well!" said Mrs Bugg, as they all trooped back to the living room. "Reckon that'll have broke the farmers' hearts! That'll be the potato tops flayed, an' the heart of the beet tore out."

"Not to mention the floodin'!" Louie piped up. "That allus git whoolly flooded down the village when there's a bad storm. Don't it, Mam?"

"That do," agreed Mrs Bugg.

Nicholas frowned. He was remembering Louie talking of flooding once before. In the woods. Why did it seem so important, suddenly, that he remember? In the woods . . . talking about the colonel . . . 'Colonel Duckworth', she had said the villagers called him. 'Duckworth' because of the flooding in the Home Guard bunker . . . The bunker!

Realization cracked through him like a whiplash. He jumped as though he had been physically struck. Slipping unnoticed into the kitchen he ran on tiptoe for the back door. The rain poked cold needles through the thin stuff of his shirt, blinding him until he took off his spectacles and shoved them into his pocket. Then he began to run—not for his own life, but for Victor's. "Drowned like a rat. Drowned like a rat." The cruel phrase stuck in the groove of his brain to torment him as he plashed his desperate way through the beaten, sodden countryside.

20

Free!

He had promised himself, as he ran, that if he were in time he would set Victor free. There was nothing else for it. He had had to cope with problem after problem, and the storm had been the last straw. He had done his best. He had saved the rat from being poisoned. Now it would have to take its chances. If he were in time . . .

He was in time! The water which was running down the sloping bank of Amos's Grove in tiny, erratic tributaries had, as yet, penetrated only the outer room of the bunker where it lay in a thin film over the floor. The inner room was still quite dry. Nicholas leaned back against the door, gasping for breath and pressing his hand to his side, until the pain of the stitch eased. Then he tugged his shirt from his trousers to wring the wet from his hair and wipe his face. There was only a faint glimmer left in the torch, but it was sufficient to show him the cage and the small, dark shape sitting expectantly at the top of the ladder. He dropped to his knees, pulled the handkerchief from his pocket, and emptied the pieces of potato on to the floor. Then he pulled Simon's gloves on, and opened the cage door.

The rat had been craving its freedom. Nicholas could tell from the way it leapt out past his arm to scuttle away from him into the blackness. He stood up slowly, so as not to frighten it, and walked over to prop the door open with the empty cage.

"There now!" he said in a choked voice. "You can eat your dinner and go." For answer there was a sudden whirring noise. Somewhere Victor was scrabbling like fury, trying to burrow down into the earthen floor of the bunker. Silly rat! Nicholas thought angrily, trying to ignore the hard ball in his throat and the smarting behind his eyes. After all I've done for him! And he's afraid to run past me!

He turned away, head bowed, and walked slowly to the

bunker's entrance. As he reached it, the torch finally died on him. Well, that's that, he thought.

The rain had eased a little. He pulled his spectacles from his left-hand pocket and put them on. Shivering, he looked down to find his shirt sticking to him like a cold plaster, and his trousers soaked black. I ought to go home, he thought. They'll be looking for me.

He could not tear himself away, though. He splashed along the track as far as the gate, walking slowly backwards in the hope of catching a last glimpse of Victor as he left the bunker. He leaned against the gate. "V for Victor. Dot, dot, dash," he chanted drearily, and wondered whether the sick, empty feeling inside him had come through his being upset, or because he had given half his dinner to Victor.

"V for . . ." The bang of the explosion roared against his eardrums. At the same time the ground rolled and bucked beneath his feet, tossing him from the track into the bushes, where he lay spreadeagled on his face under a shower of earth-pellets and stones. For a few seconds his head was full of dancing, dazzling lights. Then it cleared, and he rose shakily to his feet. What had happened? A thunderbolt? He staggered back to the track. Thick, swirling smoke was rising into the air from the direction of the bunker.

"Victor!" he screamed, and tried to force his papery legs to run towards the smoke. "Victor! I'm coming!"

He stumbled, fell and began to crawl.

Two legs appeared in front of him. He was hauled to his feet and dragged back along the way he had come. "Run, bor! Run!" Simon Bugg's hoarse voice yelled in his ear.

Nicholas wriggled out of his grasp. "No!" he cried. "Victor's in there! I have to save him!"

Miraculously his legs found strength. He began to run, making long strides.

"For God's sake!" Simon yelled after him. "That's explosives in there!"

The second bang seemed, for a second, to split Nicholas's head in two. Then a warm, rushing wind picked him up and bore him along. It dropped him, face down, on to a bed of flints. There was a searing pain in his chest, and he closed his eyes. When he opened them a skeleton, open-armed and grinning, was rising from the earth to embrace him. He began to shriek and then to wail in a long, high, terrified monotone, that sang through his head, gradually fading, as he slipped into a soft, black oblivion.

When he opened his eyes the second time, he was lying at the side of the track, covered in an old, grey army blanket, and with his head on Simon Bugg's knees. He sat up slowly, helped by the man's supporting arm.

"You give me some scare!" said Simon. "Thought you was a goner! That were jest a faint, though, an' a bit of a cut on your head from your specs when they broke. I've bandaged that with your hanky." His voice was very kind, like Mrs Bugg's.

"What was it?" Nicholas moaned. "What happened?"

"Don't rightly know," said Simon. " 'Cept that there must of bin some kind of explosives in the bunker. That sound like nitro to me. Ruddy fools musta had that buried an' forgot it were there."

"Victor was digging . . ." Nicholas began, then slumped forward as the full force of his grief hit him. He cried very hard for a bit; then, as his sobs subsided, he realized Simon was talking to him.

"That wouldn't suffer no pain, little 'un," he was saying earnestly. "Do you listen to what I tell you now! 'Cos it's true! That'd be diggin'. Then, 'Pop!' That'd be jest as though it'd fell asleep."

"But I killed him all the same," said Nicholas thickly, wiping the back of his hand across his eyes.

"You saved him from a nasty, sufferin' death," Simon said firmly. "Rat-catcher'd hev got him some time or another. An' look what you give him! Food. An' comfort. Then his freedom. For he's free now. An' that were jest as if he'd fell asleep. So don't you go a-grievin' for him no more!"

Nicholas stood up groggily and handed Simon his blanket.

101

"I'll have to go home," he said. "I'll be in dreadful trouble as it is."

"I'd bes' take you," Simon said. "Carry you piggyback. Bring in the wounded like we done in the army, an' report to the officers. Bes' let me tell 'em 'bout your little old rat, bor!"

"All right," said Nicholas gratefully.

From somewhere behind them, in the direction of the bunker, came the sound of shouting.

"That'll be old Duckworth down from the Hall, rememberin' 'bout his nitro at las'," said Simon scornfully. "Let's you an' me git out of it quick!"

All the way home, as Nicholas bobbed up and down on his back, swathed in the grey blanket, Simon talked in his hoarse, kind voice, repeating the same things over and over. How Victor would have felt no pain. How comfortable Nicholas had made him in his cage in the bunker. How lucky he had been to have been saved from the rat-catcher's poison. It was like a healing bandage being wrapped around Nicholas's heart.

"But what was the worst moment? The very worst moment?" Morna asked again that night before they went to sleep. She was perched cross-legged on the end of Nicholas's bed, hugging Anastasia.

"I've told you ten times," grumbled Nicholas who still had a slight headache.

"Just once more! Please!" pleaded Morna.

"It was when the skeleton sat up and tried to pull me into the ground," said Nicholas.

"And it grinned at you?"

"Yes! You know that!"

"It didn't really happen. Did it?" Morna said, suddenly changing her tone and assuming a superior smile. "It was just like one of your nightmares. All in your head."

"I don't know," said Nicholas. "It seemed very real."

"But you didn't tell Aunt Dorothy about it!"

"I know," said Nicholas. "I thought she might worry. And Mrs Bugg says she's not very practised at worrying."

102

"She will be by the time you leave her," Morna pointed out, as she leapt over to her own bed.

Nicholas lay down and closed his eyes. Just as he began to drift into sleep, though, he struggled up again.

"Morna," he said. "You don't think Louie would break her promise and tell anyone else about Victor? Mrs Bugg says the villagers might turn nasty if they heard I'd been feeding a rat."

"Of course Louie won't break her promise!" said Morna. "She's a very honourable person!"

"That's all right, then," said Nicholas, lying down again.

"I suppose it all turned out quite well, considering," Morna said reflectively. "I mean your finding Simon Bugg, and his talking at last, and everything . . . though I'm sure I don't know why you risked your life for a rat. I think that was insane!"

"Can't you understand anything?" muttered Nicholas crossly. "He was Victor! He was my friend!"

21

Found Out?

Aunt Dorothy insisted that Nicholas stay in bed on Wednesday in case of delayed concussion.

"I expect she's really punishing you," Morna remarked as she dressed. "You almost made her faint yesterday, you know, when you arrived on Simon's back with that bandage round your head. I shouldn't think she feels very kindly towards you."

"Yesterday was the saddest day of my life," said Nicholas shakily. "I don't see why I should be punished for it."

"Who's being punished?" asked Aunt Dorothy in an astonished voice. She had arrived with Nicholas's breakfast, and he could see immediately that she had taken a great deal of care over it. She had given him the china 'squirrel' eggcup, the

Chinese bone spoon (over which he and Morna always squabbled) and the ivory-handled knife for quartering his orange.

"No one's going to be punished," she said kindly, "but someone might be a little spoiled!"

Indeed for the rest of the day Nicholas was treated like a pampered invalid. Morna and Louie were banned from the bedroom because they were too noisy. Mrs Bugg brought him in biscuits and drinks. And Aunt Dorothy appeared at regular intervals to plump up his pillows and make sure he was generally comfortable and not bored. Had it not been for the memory of Victor, like a bruise on his heart which made him wince whenever he probed it, he would have felt quite cheerful, in spite of being confined to bed.

After lunch Simon Bugg came in to see him. "Brought you some news, bor!" he announced, perching uneasily on the edge of Morna's bed. "That explosion were jes' what I thought. Nitro! 'Parently them Home Guard guerrillas, what Cutworth was in charge of, buried it under the bunker in 1941. In three milk churns that was! That's the talk of the village today. Folks is ragin'! Sayin' that could've blown someone sky-high."

"But aren't they wondering what set the explosion off?" Nicholas asked anxiously after he had digested this piece of information.

"They think it were the storm," Simon told him.

After scrutinizing Nicholas sharply for a moment, he rose to go, pausing at the door to say gently, "Now don't you go worritin' none, little 'un! Nor grievin' neither. Remember what I told you."

"Yes. I do," Nicholas assured him.

He felt a warm surge of affection for Simon Bugg. Aunt Dorothy, Morna, and Mrs Bugg had all been very kind to him. But Nicholas felt that Simon was the only one who really understood what he had felt for Victor. And although Simon did not talk nearly as much as the others, what he did say was always comforting and to the point. He could not think why he had ever felt afraid of him.

He was with Simon in the vegetable garden the following morning (for Aunt Dorothy had allowed him out on condition that he did not play any strenuous games) when Morna came running down the path, panting and crimson-cheeked. She had just returned from shopping and obviously had some news for them.

"You look as though your eyes are going to pop out," Nicholas told her.

"Do be quiet, Nick!" she said impatiently. "This is really important! There are notices up everywhere about an emergency meeting tomorrow morning at ten o'clock in the village hall. Mrs Nelson says it's about the explosion."

Simon stopped hoeing and turned to stare at Morna. "What about the explosion?" he asked.

"I don't know," said Morna, frowning. "Only it's very important. So we must go. Aunt Dorothy says so, too. Everyone except Nick, of course. He might not be feeling well enough for a meeting."

Nicholas gave a strained little smile to show that he had heard the reference to himself. He was watching an ant make a circuitous journey round the clods of earth between the bean rows. At the same time another ant seemed to be threading its way through his brain, writing the same message over and over: 'They've found me out . . . They've found me out!' He hardly knew what he was doing during the next fifteen minutes. He moved automatically, following the others into elevenses, sitting down at the table, drinking his tea. He sat like a rock while the waves of conversation washed over his head. The others were discussing the possible reasons for the village meeting.

"I reckon ol' Duckworth's goin' to 'pologize to us all," Mrs Bugg said happily, as she went round the table refilling their cups.

"Pigs'll come flyin' over when that happen!" Simon remarked gruffly.

"Perhaps they've discovered some more caches of explosives," Aunt Dorothy suggested. "The soldiers have been

105

down in the wood since Wednesday morning."

"The village might have to be evacuated if they have," Morna pointed out, adding, "Where would we all go?"

"Over to Aunt Connie's," said Simon. "She got two old hen-houses she don't use."

Everyone laughed very heartily at this because it was Simon's first attempt at a joke since he had started to talk again. Nicholas laughed, too. But underneath his laughter he was wriggling miserably and wondering why none of the others had guessed, as he had, the real reason for the meeting.

That afternoon he went inside of his own accord to lie on his bed and try to sort out his thoughts. To begin with he wondered about who might have betrayed him. Certainly not Aunt Dorothy. It could have been any of the others, though. Not that they would have done it intentionally. But Morna, for instance, talked very loudly when she was excited and she might have been discussing Victor with Louie and have been overheard. Or Mrs Bugg, who sometimes rattled on at great length, might easily have let Nicholas's secret out without even realizing she had done so! There was Louie, too. She could have told Tommy. After all, he was her brother, and they were quite close in a funny sort of way . . .

As though she had read his thoughts Louie suddenly peered round the door. When she saw that Nicholas was awake she tiptoed into the room, whispering, " 'Scuse me, little 'un. But I'm jes' hidin' up, 'cos old Grim-fizz is at the door talkin' to your auntie an' Morna."

"What does he want?" asked Nicholas, sitting up.

"He's on about that old meetin'. How he want you all to be there," Louie told him.

A moment later the front door closed and, with a cheerful wave, Louie was gone.

Nicholas propped himself up on one elbow and gnawed at his thumb. If his suspicions had needed confirming the headmaster's visit had done so. There was surely no doubt now about the purpose of the meeting. The unmasking of a rat-lover! The exposing of an enemy of the people! He was already known in the village as a shirt-ripper. Now he would be the boy who had fed precious food to a rat and blown up part of Saxford, too. He could imagine all too vividly what would take place in the hall tomorrow morning. All those angry Saxford faces turning round to look for him. Where was he, they would be asking. Where was Nicholas Newton? He saw himself rise from his chair and walk slowly forward. It would be horrific: like walking into flames! But he would have to do it. He was a Newton. Nicholas Newton. No one would say he was a shirker!

"All right, Sir Nicholas?" Aunt Dorothy was looking in anxiously from the lobby. "The girls said you were lying down."

"Yes. I'm all right, thank you," Nicholas said staunchly. "I wanted to read, but it was too noisy outside."

He fished *The Wind in the Willows* from under his bed and made a pretence of reading it until Aunt Dorothy had gone. Then he threw it dispiritedly on to the floor and flopped face down on his pillow. It was at a time like this that he missed Nooka sorely.

22

A Legend Exploded

By five minutes to ten on Friday morning the hall was crowded. There were even people standing along the two side passages and in the space between the door and the last row of chairs. Nicholas was sitting between Simon Bugg and Aunt Dorothy in the third back row, six seats in from the centre aisle. Morna was between Aunt Dorothy and Mrs Bugg, with Louie and Tommy on their mother's other side.

Nicholas felt very calm and very odd. It may have been to do with the fact that he was still without spectacles and had returned to his former misted world again. Whatever the

107

reason, it was as though the real Nicholas were floating high
overhead among the cobwebbed rafters, looking detachedly
down on the Nicholas Newton who would shortly be the
object of the villagers' fury.

The bee-like murmur in the hall died suddenly. "Grimes!"
muttered Simon, and Nicholas could see a tall figure on the
platform gesticulating for silence.

"I'm glad to see a full house," Mr Grimes began in his
clipped, precise voice. "I have a very important announcement
to make, and I shall do it as briefly as possible, because I know
Friday morning is a busy time for most of you . . ."

In the pause that followed had a feather dropped to the floor
it might have been heard. Nicholas was aware of a pain beginning low down in his belly. How terrible if he had to rush out
to the lavatory just as Mr Grimes told what he had done! They
would all think he was running away.

"I expect you all know that a party of Royal Engineers has
been inspecting the site of Tuesday's explosion," Mr Grimes
continued. "Well, the fact is they've found something . . ." He
paused again, and an impatient voice from the middle of the
hall called out, "What?"

It sounded, Nicholas thought, like Mr Ward. He wriggled.
The belt of pain had tightened, as though drawn in a notch.
What could the soldiers have found, he asked himself. The
remains of Victor's cage? Victor's body?

"They have found a skeleton, my good man," said Mr
Grimes, in a tone that showed he disliked being interrupted.
"They have found a skeleton in Amos's Grove. And, beside it,
a metal box containing a quantity of Victorian coins!"

There were gasps, exclamations, and an agitated murmur.

"Quiet, please!" Mr Grimes said sharply.

Nicholas's pain subsided.

"Home Office experts have been called in," continued Mr
Grimes, talking more rapidly now that he had made the de-
sired impact on his audience. "They are agreed that the
skeleton is almost certainly that of Abraham Footer. There
also seems little doubt that the unfortunate man was a victim

108

of the earthquake which occurred on April 22nd, 1884. The earth must literally have opened and swallowed him up . . ."

Another murmurous wave rose and fell.

"There were similar instances reported of fissures opening and closing in just this way along the Essex coast. People who saw this phenomenon have remembered it with horror all their days. Is it any wonder that a man who saw his companion disappear in such a fearful way should have collapsed and died of a heart attack or a stroke?"

The hall seethed. Simon muttered a low, "Corblast!" Nicholas, feeling suddenly light-headed, gripped the edge of his chair until the sensation had passed. Mr Grimes stamped his foot three times for silence. When all was quiet he said, slowly and loudly, "Amos Bugg was not murdered. He died of natural causes. From this day let the feud die also!"

No one spoke or even whispered. An unnatural silence had fallen. Nicholas waited, tense with excitement, for the cheers and the clapping which must eventually break it. When the fracturing voice did come, though, it was a woman's asking matter-of-factly, "So what's going' to happen to all that money they foun', Headmaster? That mus' be worth a tidy bit!"

"That," said Mr Grimes shortly as he withdrew from the platform, "is a matter for the parish council, Madam."

There was a scraping of chairs, and the hall began to empty.

"Well!" exclaimed Mrs Bugg, leaning forward to look along at them all. "Well, I never! I'm that flabbergasted I can't hardly think of nothin' to say!"

"I thought all the Buggs and the Footers would run over to one another and shake hands!" Morna said, her voice sharp with disappointment. "That's what people do in stories when they're reconciled."

"You got a hope, my old love!" said Mrs Bugg with a short laugh. "Reckon that'll take ten year to git them a-speakin' to one another."

"Still, I expect the fighting will stop," Aunt Dorothy observed, turning to give Nicholas a particularly warm smile.

"That will," agreed Mrs Bugg. "But gradual. Like when you pull a weed out by the root, Mrs Buchanan. That live for a bit on the surface, 'fore that die of starvation."

Simon rose suddenly, pushed silently past them, and joined the queue filing out.

"Gradual that'll be," Mrs Bugg whispered. "Like with our Simon. Can't 'spect no miracles overnight."

"Mam!" Tommy wailed petulantly. "Louie hit me!"

" 'Cos he say he won't stop fightin' Footers, Mam!" Louie explained hurriedly.

"He'll stop," declared Mrs Bugg, standing up and pulling Louie and Tommy to their feet. "Or I'll know the reason why! Now, let's git off 'fore we miss that Bury bus."

"Come on, chickens," said Aunt Dorothy to Morna and Nicholas. "Time to go home!"

At half past eleven Morna and Nicholas found themselves alone for the first time that morning. They had just finished their milk and biscuits and were now wandering aimlessly around the orchard.

"So!" said Morna suddenly, with an embarrassed little laugh. "I suppose you feel quite proud of yourself!"

"Why?" asked Nicholas.

"Well, it's all happened because of you, hasn't it? Even though they don't know it in the village. You've saved them all—like Joan of Arc."

"If I had done it, I would have been like King Arthur, not Joan," said Nicholas. "But I didn't. It was Victor. He gave his life." He watched Morna suspiciously.

After a minute, however, when she had neither laughed nor made a scornful remark, he relaxed. "Come with me," he said. "I've something to show you."

He led her down to the bottom of the orchard to a spot in front of the fence where a wooden cross had been sunk into the earth. On the cross-bar was a small running rat, on the upright the letter 'V'.

"Simon did that for me," he said. "He taught himself to

110

carve in the prison camp. Do you like it?"

"Yes," said Morna decidedly. "I could bring wild flowers to lay in front of it every day."

He nodded his approval silently. Then Morna turned abruptly to stare towards the cottage and Nicholas saw her stiffen. "What is it?" he asked.

"The rat-catcher," she whispered. "I'd forgotten this was his day."

They stood silently in front of the cross while Mr Bullace came and went. As the van finally moved away from the gate, they exchanged a conspiratorial smile.

All at once Nicholas felt deliciously, absurdly happy. He was a giant! If he leaped he could touch the sky. If he tugged he could pull up a tree. He began to gallop round the orchard, springing up to catch the branches.

"What is it?" Morna cried excitedly, running behind him. "Is it a game?"

"Follow-my-leader!" he yelled over his shoulder. "I'm crazy! I'm insane! And I'm leader this round!"

"You're leader this round!" Morna agreed, shrieking with laughter as she leaped after him through the trees.